dancing in the rain

BY LYNN JOSEPH

Blouse and Skirt Books, Kingsto.

© Lynn Joseph 2016
Dancing in the Rain

First published in Kingston by Blouse & Skirt Books, 2016

Blouse & Skirt Books is an imprint of Blue Moon Publishing

A CIP catalogue record of this book is available from the National Library of
Jamaica

ISBN 978-976-95436-9-0

Cover Design by Nucleus Creative

Blue Moon Publishing
PO Box 5464
Liguanea PO
Kingston 6
Jamaica, W.I.

www.blumoonbooks.com

Thanks are due to CODE, The Burt Award for Caribbean Literature and the
Bocas Literary Festival

For Brandt Scott, who, at eight years old, drew a picture for me and wrote on it, "Be Free! Be Strong! Be Yourself!" It hung on my refrigerator for many years. Words to live by.

Thank you, son.

Acknowledgements

AMONG THE MANY who lost their lives on September 11, were hundreds of citizens from over 90 countries, including islands in the Caribbean. It is reported that 47 Dominicans from the Dominican Republic were among those who lost their lives that day. This story is my attempt to glimpse the impact of this global tragedy on two families: in the Dominican Republic and in New York.

This story is also very personal for me. On September 11, 2001, I was a trial lawyer heading to federal court with my trial partner, Patricia Miller, in downtown New York City, just two blocks from the World Trade Center. The events that day changed my entire life. I witnessed with many others, in shock and disbelief, the devastating sight and loud explosions of the first American Airlines plane hitting the North Tower of the World Trade Center. Then came the terror and fear of trying to escape Manhattan Island by walking across the Brooklyn Bridge as both Towers behind us bled clouds of smoke and debris.

My first thank you is to Patricia Miller, now Chief of the Special Federal Litigation Division of NYC's Law Department, for immediately alerting staff at our nearby office to evacuate the building, and for getting us both off that island before the towers collapsed. Thank you, Pat. I honestly don't know what I'd have done without you by my side during the most overwhelmingly horrific day of my life.

I also want to thank Amanda Jenkins, my first advisor at the Vermont College of Fine Arts, who recognized that I needed to write about this traumatic experience and gently (ha!) urged me to do so. Thank you also to my VCFA workshop friends and leaders, with whom I shared the beginning of this story while I held my breath so I wouldn't cry.

Thank you to the Canadian education NGO, CODE, for recognizing that this story has merit and awarding it a generous Burt Literary Award for Caribbean literature at the 2015 Bocas Literary Festival in Trinidad.

Thank you to John Spellman, who let me camp out at his kitchen table for days while I finished writing the story in time to enter the Burt competition, and who kept me going with his great meals.

Thank you to the amazingly talented, insightful and inspiring editor/publisher, Tanya Batson-Savage, who did everything right in creating this book with me, from the cover to the content! You are truly an award-winning publisher and I wish every writer had an editor like you.

Thank you to my bestie, Eva Martinez, for being the back-up (and sometimes the main) mom to my sons, and for making us all go horse back riding in the Dominican Republic on that memorable day that now lives on in this story.

Thank you to Jose Severino, who is, and always will be, my Dominican family, and to Baz Dreisinger for being a sister/friend with a permanent home wherever I am.

Thank you to my son Jared, who is my heart, even though we are so very different and I hate video games. Thank you for trying to call me on September 11. I love you honey! And of course, thank you to my son Brandt, for being the everlasting joy in my and many other people's lives.

Lastly, to Andre Daly, my best friend and companion in all things happy and sad, joyful and painful. Thank you for always turning on the light when I'm in the dark.

prologue

THROW OPEN THE WINDOWS to Doña Maria's front room and Sosúa Bay glitters like butterfly wings tipped in silver. I want to run outside and glide like a mermaid into the waves. But I have three more rooms to clean and I don't think Doña Maria would be too happy if I decided to dive into the sea. Doña Maria never thinks about butterflies or mermaids or even the sea although it's right here in front of her face. Doña Maria sees only the inside of a sad heart.

I hear the waves knocking on the door of her big, green house begging Doña Maria to come out. And I see the way Doña Maria pulls the curtains tight across the windows and how she covers her ears with her hands to block out the song of the sea.

"How sad to not listen to the sea," I tell my Mamí one day as she washes the thick, white towels that Doña Maria insists must be washed by hand. "How terrible to turn your back on the friend who comes calling every day and night begging to see you and you won't even talk to him."

Mamí gives me an odd look. "I don't know how I have a child like you, talking so funny and thinking strange things when there is so much work to do."

"But Mamí," I say, "can't you hear the sea calling for her. I can hear it even when I am on the other side of the house asleep in our bed."

"Doña Maria has troubles we will never know about," Mamí says, handing me one end of a towel to wring.

"Like what?" I ask.

But Mamí shakes her head. I know there won't be any more talking as we work. Mamí ignores Doña Maria's sadness although it's there standing up tall and strong in every room of the big house.

Still, when the sea is glittering like this, I hurry up and sweep the dark wood floors and mop them with a heavy cloth of wax. Then I put a bowl of mangoes on the long dining room table and vases of pink hibiscuses on each side of it. Finally, I'm finished and I whirl around the table as a yellow butterfly chases me.

"Qué pasa, Elizabeth?"

Doña Maria is standing at the heavy door with her hands on her hips. She is really my tía, my Mamí's half-sister, and she looks like my Mamí. Even though she is family, we call her Doña Maria because she married a rich sea captain and travelled all over the world and now she owns this casa grande by the sea and we work for her.

I stop in the middle of a twirl. The yellow butterfly flitters fast out the window. "Hola, Señora," I curtsey. I smooth back my hair and straighten my dress. "I was just working in here."

"Dancing is not working. Please continue quietly, Elizabeth."

"Sí, Doña Maria," I speak so softly that she looks at me suspiciously.

Doña Maria turns to go and then she stops and looks at the flowers I have placed on the table. "Don't forget to close that window," she says, before walking away.

I wait until Doña Maria leaves then I run outside dropping my dust cloths on the back steps. There is a little sea next to the backyard. It is not the strong swirling sea that lives in front of Doña Maria's big house, but a sweet, small cove where the water nestles into a pool like a curled blue ribbon and feathery trees drip yellow blossoms on the rocks. Here, even the saddest person could find happiness if they ever bothered to look.

I walk slowly into the pool feeling the cool water around my ankles and knees. Then, I let out a loud whoop and splash all the way in. This is where I sing and dance and throw up my arms. This is where Doña Maria's sadness does not touch me. It is where I can breathe again. The sadness is waiting for me too. I can feel it coming. Every day it gets stronger and bigger and soon it will steal my soul and I will never dance again.

"Elizabeth, ven acá!" It's Mamí calling me to come quickly. "A storm is coming."

The sky is changing fast. Black clouds fly over Mt. Isabel like dark-winged birds. Overhead, the sun is still shining but the white clouds and the blue sky are disappearing. When the sun is shining like this and the rain is coming at the same time, they say a bruja, a witch, is getting married.

I love these storms. The waves rise up like roaring giants from out of the sea. They race in and smash against the rocks, and then fling themselves, broken and shattered, high into the sky. They fill up my little pool with presents of spiral shells and smooth black stones from the bottom of the sea.

"Elizabeth?" calls Mamí, as she comes into our bedroom. I am leaning out the window letting the rain fall on my hands.

"Mamí, can I go outside in the rain, please. I promise Doña Maria won't see."

Mamí's face darkens. "No, mi amor."

I don't know why, but ever since we moved into Doña Maria's big, green house Mamí will not let me go outside during the storms. I can no longer dance under the raindrops or spin in the wind. I can only watch everything from this window and pretend that life has stopped.

Mamí walks out the room with a backward glance that says, "You better listen."

I lean my chin on the window again and watch the storm swirling and dancing until the heavy clouds turn into night. That's when I hear the deep heavy rumble of a voice saying, "Ven acá, ven acá."

I tiptoe past Mamí sewing in the kitchen, past the living room, and down the long hallway to the front of the house where Doña Maria lives. I'm not supposed to go there after my work is done, but that voice is getting louder and louder. "Ven acá!" Come here! It sounds like a loud cry.

I see Doña Maria standing in the dining room where my pink hibiscuses have disappeared. I imagine that the sea king came and took them and I smile at the thought of the great sea king wearing my pink flowers in his beard.

"Do you hear it?" she asks in a frightened voice. Her eyes are now looking straight ahead at the closed windows. And from behind the curtained windows I can hear the sea calling to Doña Maria.

"Yes," I say. The sea's voice is deep and sad just like Doña Maria's. I stay frozen in my spot watching her.

"Doña Maria," I whisper, but the sound of the sea drowns out my voice. I don't know if it's the magic of the storm that makes me want to break this sadness, but I speak up loud and clear. "Doña Maria, open the window. The sea is calling you."

Doña Maria stands there not moving one inch.

She doesn't answer, but she does a very strange thing. She takes my hand and holds it tightly. I look up to see if this is the same cold, distant Doña Maria I know. But I see nothing at all because the lights go out and we are covered in darkness.

Suddenly, a window crashes open and wind is swirling around blowing the curtains this way and that and Doña Maria is squeezing my hand so tightly I want to scream with pain but I don't. I let her hold on to me and I listen as the sea king enters the room through the blown-away curtains and the wide-open window. From under the darkness, the sea's voice is sharp and commanding and I tremble because I can hear the words and it is definitely calling, *Doña Maria, come to me. Come to me, Doña Maria,* and I hold her hand tightly so she won't have to go because now I am sorry I told her to open the window.

I don't know how long Doña Maria and I stand there holding hands as the sea begs her to come. The windows rattle. Wet, salt spray mists over our faces.

"I thought it was a friend," I whisper to her.

"It's my husband," she replies. I know without a doubt that Doña Maria is telling the truth. Doña Maria is a statue, and I don't know what to do.

Doña Maria takes a step toward the open window and then another. She reaches her arms toward the wind and sea. Suddenly, I don't care that she is Doña Maria and that she is our rich tía with a fancy name and house and that she pays for our food and clothes. I drag her across the room, pulling her hands and body as hard as I can until she is leaning on me and I bend under her weight.

She is heavy, but I am strong. I have carried buckets of water up and down many steps. I have wrung dripping wet towels to hang on clotheslines. I have even carried baskets of papayas and mangoes on my head to sell on the beach before we came to live with Doña Maria.

Doña Maria says nothing at all as I half-carry, half-drag her out of the dining room and down the long corridor to the big kitchen where tall candles send beams of light dancing across the ceiling. Mamí is still sitting in her rocking chair, sewing. Her basket of threads is in her lap. When she sees us she jumps up with a shout. "Mi hermana!" The coloured threads fall to the floor and tangle up like fishing lines or forgotten memories. Before she can say anything else I speak fast.

"Mamí, Doña Maria would like some café con leche, por favor. And a warm blanket. She is wet from the rain."

"Sí, claro que sí," says Mamí, hurrying to the stove with milk and coffee.

I take Doña Maria over to the rocking chair and help her sit down. Then I place the blanket Mamí hands me around her shoulders. I sit on a stool next to her and hold her hand and we wait for the café. No one says anything as Doña Maria drinks the hot sweet coffee and rocks back and forth in the chair. Her face is pale and her long hair has fallen out of its usual twist on the back of her neck. Her hair flutters all around her shoulders. Under the candlelight, her hair looks just like the silver-tipped wings of the sea.

"Doña Maria." I whisper, "you have butterfly wings." I hold up strands of her hair and they shimmer. "Look at your wings, Tía. That means you can dance on the waves. You don't have to drown in them."

Tía looks at her silvery hair falling through my fingertips. Her dark eyes brighten as she looks right into my eyes and says softly, "Yes, Elizabeth, I see."

1

brandt
FLOATING IN THE SKY

N THE LAST DAY OF SUMMER vacation, Mommy takes me and Jared to lunch at her job in one of the tallest buildings in New York. Jared doesn't want to go. He wants to stay home and play games on the computer. Mostly, he goes to the Neopets website and creates virtual pets because we can't have any real ones in our two bedroom apartment. He chats online to friends he does not know, sends instant messages to kids far away, and ignores me as I watch television.

"Jared, look at this big escalator, you want to run down the up?"

Jared shakes his head at me with a disgusted look on his face. It's the look that says, "Don't bother me, I'm busy," as he thumbs away at his Gameboy, walking with his head down.

"Jared, don't ignore your brother," Mommy says in her tight voice.

Jared doesn't answer her and I see Mommy's face getting red. I take her hand and squeeze it. "You wanna run up the down?"

Mommy laughs, just like I knew she would. I could always make her forget she's mad at Jared, which she seems to be all the time. Mommy thinks that Jared doesn't notice her counting under her breath, or pressing her lips together tightly, or clenching her fists hard, but he does. And it makes him feel like he's wrong. All the time.

It's not easy being Jared. It's very easy being me though. I love everything. If Mommy wants to take us to lunch at her job, I think about the cool stuff there, starting with the escalators, then the security men in their black uniforms who sing along to a radio on their desks, then the elevator ride to the tip top and then, presto, the gleaming restaurant, filled with table cloths and flowers and most of all windows. Tall, clear windows that look like air. When I get close to them and press my head on the window, I feel like I'm floating in the sky.

"Jared, I'm an astronaut!" I say, my arms spread wide and I walk as if I'm floating on air.

I see a little smile on the corner of Jared's lips, but he doesn't answer. He glances out the window from under his lashes and takes in the view of the other tall matching silver building, and the river and bridges far below us. He's taking a photograph of it all with his amazing brain. Later, he will tell me all the details I missed.

"The light is making everything glittery like the sea," I tell Mommy.

She smiles. That's the kind of thing she likes to hear. "Wow, Brandt, you're right. It does. What an observant boy you are!"

Jared smirks. "Is it outer space or the ocean, make up your mind."

Mommy tells Jared to hush. "Let him use his imagination. At least he's not stuck in a game all the time."

Jared's lips clamp shut.

"This is supposed to be fun, mister," Mommy takes Jared's game from him. Mommy has no idea how much Jared sees and hears while he's playing his game. She doesn't know that Jared has fun all by himself. He doesn't need lunch or tall buildings in the sky for that.

Without his Gameboy Jared leans back in his chair and stares out the window. I want to tell him a joke and make him laugh. My brother has the funnest laugh ever. His entire face changes like a great song turned up on high volume.

"We're sitting next to Heaven," I say.

Jared rolls his eyes, but at least he's not staring out angry and silent anymore.

Mommy waves to the waiter in a white shirt and black pants who looks like he's going to a party. It's Mr. Hernández, Mommy's friend from back home.

"Hola mi amigos!"

Mommy starts talking fast Spanish to him. They are both from Sosúa, the same town in the Dominican Republic. Every other word is an excited, 'mi pais', as if their country belongs just to them. I see Mr. Hernández whenever we come to eat here with Mommy. He gives me little presents like once he wrapped up a tiny shrimp fork for me to take home.

Mr. Hernández tells us in English that he's excited to go back home and see his daughter next week. "My angel," he tells Mommy, who nods and looks at me. She doesn't glance at Jared.

"I wish I could go back home, too," Mommy says with a frog sound in her voice.

"Oh, but you should go! Take your hijos." He touches Jared's arm to pull him into the conversation.

"No Dominicano should ever stay so long from home, it's like a fish out of water, or a . . ." He looks out of the tall windows behind us. "A bird out of the sky."

"A computer without memory," Jared mutters.

"A tiger out of the jungle," I add.

"A boy without his Gameboy." Jared giggles.

"A face without a smile." I stick my tongue out at him.

He kicks me under the table and a fork falls to the floor. "A baby without his mama."

"Enough!" Mommy says.

But it's my turn. "A lunch without dessert."

Jared bursts out laughing and then I do, too.

Mommy won't say anything mean to me. I'm the baby. I'm the easy child. I've heard her say that a hundred times. And so has Jared.

Being me is easy, but being Mommy's easy child is very hard. It's a life sentence for my brother.

We place our orders and eat our last day of summer lunch as dark clouds swirl by.

Mr. Hernandez gives us a special dessert of chocolate pudding that he calls mousse. "A storm is coming," he says.

"I love this chocolate mouse!"

Jared growls, "Grow up."

"Be nice to your brother, Jared."

Jared's glare turns icy cold.

Rain begins to fall hitting the windows in hard, fast drops. The sky has disappeared.

I make a chocolate mustache with my dessert but Jared doesn't laugh again.

"Is normalmente," Mr. Hernández says to Mommy. "Kids are like that. Sometimes you have to, cómo se dice? Ignore them!

"Ignore him?" Mommy answers in her most irritated voice that she uses for late trains, cold food, and Jared. "I can't ignore him. He'll only get worse."

"Well then," says Mr. Hernández, straightening his white apron that is spotless and neatly ironed. "Ignore yourself."

"Cómo?" Mommy flicks crumbs on the tablecloth. "I don't understand."

"My hija in Sosúa say strange things but I tell myself, 'Danielo, you don't know what she knows.' So I ignore how I feel and I let her just be her."

Mommy stares at his back as he walks off whistling a merengue tune that I have heard on the radio at home.

Jared smiles a strange smile. Like he just won points in a game.

Before Mommy can decide if to ignore Mr. Hernández's advice, he comes hurrying back to our table. He holds out a plate with a chunk of cake and a candle lit up brightly in the creamy centre. "Here, make a wish."

"But it's not my birthday," says Mommy.

Mr. Hernández nods. "There doesn't have to be a reason to make a wish. My hija taught me that."

He waits for Mommy to blow out the candle but she shakes her head. "It's weird." She glances around the restaurant at all the fancy people watching us to see what the special occasion is.

Mr. Hernández picks up the plate and sets it in front of Jared. "Here, son, make a wish."

Jared stares at the cake all suspicious and skeptical just like Mommy and I want to laugh because he and Mommy have the exact same looks on their faces but they cannot see it.

I clap my hands. "I'll blow it out."

Mr. Hernández puts the cake in front of me and leaves to help other guests. I close my eyes and make my wish.

"Stop!" I hear Mommy shriek.

My eyes fly open to see that Jared has stuck a finger in the frosting. He raises his eyebrows at me. "Stop being such a goody two-shoes." Then, he puts his finger in his mouth and licks it clean.

Mommy huffs crossly, "Why do you always have to spoil everything?"

Our table gets very quiet. Even I have nothing to say.

Jared plays with his napkin. Mommy stares at her cell phone, which is not ringing or beeping or anything.

"Look." I point out the window.

In between the dark clouds and rain, a yellow balloon is floating in the sky. It looks like it's dancing.

"Maybe it's going to the stars," I say.

"Or the moon," says Jared.

Mommy takes a deep breath and drops her shoulders.

"Maybe to the sun," she adds hopefully.

And my wish comes true.

2

elizabeth
SONG OF THE MERMAID

T LEAST ONCE A YEAR, in every Dominican family, a special relative arrives from the United States with presents of soaps and chocolates, sneakers, cell phones and most of all with a hint of the exciting life in Nueva York.

For me and Mamí, it is Papí who we wait for each year like we wait for Christmas. The weeks leading up to his arrival are filled with special preparations – washing windows, painting walls with scuff marks, sewing new curtains, polishing shoes and fingernails until they shine like the full moon. And finally, one day I wake up and I think, "Papí is coming today on the silver bird from heaven."

It is August and Papí has his vacation from his job as a waiter in the beautiful restaurant on top of one of the tallest buildings in New York City. He showed me pictures last year of the buildings that look like twin bridges to the sky.

Maybe he'll bring me a special doll or a brand new radio, but definitely he'll have a beautiful dress for Mamí. Pink is her favourite colour. I think of my Papí in a black suit with thick brown hair, laughing eyes, and shiny black shoes. In his pockets are pesos to hand to everyone he sees, because he is happy to be back home sharing the riches of New York.

"Papí is coming today!" I shout, and I jump out of my bed before the sun rises over Mt. Isabel de Torres.

Mamí smiles, "Buenos días," and hands me a cup of tea and a piece of fried breadfruit to eat.

Jose, Doña Maria's chofer, has brought the truck to the front of the house to carry Mamí and me to the airport where we will wait until Papí arrives with his big smile and wide-open arms and his loud voice singing, "Oh, I miss my beautiful país, and my beautiful esposa and hija."

Yes, Papí is coming and for two weeks everything will be perfect. Mamí will smile all the time and even dance a bachata or two with Papí in the backyard near the yellow blossom tree and I will watch from my window as they kiss under the blue stars.

By the time Mamí is ready to go, I am dressed in my stiff-as-a-pin yellow dress with yellow socks and white sandals and I have two yellow ribbons waving at the ends of my braids.

"Mamí, Mamí," I shout. "What do you think Papí will bring us from New York?"

"Hush, muchacha," she says, with a frown. "Don't ask what Papí will bring you? Your Papí works hard and he needs a nice quiet daughter. You will scare him away with all this shouting."

"No, Mamí," I tell her. "Papí will be happy to hear my voice. I'm going to sing him lots of songs."

Mamí looks beautiful for the trip to the airport. Her dress is like the mermaid's song, soft and silky, and when she walks it rises above her knees and flutters in the breeze.

The airport is crowded with people waiting for the big silver bird to arrive from New York. Men in baseball caps drink Presidente beer and laugh loudly, slapping each other on the shoulder and reaching into coolers for more beer. Women dressed fancy like Mamí open and close their purses, looking for handkerchiefs to wipe their noses. They are all waiting for husbands or boyfriends. Children chase each other around the poles probably wondering, like me, what new toy their Papí or uncle or abuelos will bring them from the States.

We see the plane far away in the sky long before it arrives at the airport. It's a magical speck in the blueness and it gets bigger and bigger as we point and shout and chase each other faster and faster, and the men drink more and more, and the women clutch their purses tightly, too excited now to care about handkerchiefs or noses.

Mamí squeezes my hand.

"Almost here, mi amor," she says. Her hands are wet and cold, like she has a fever.

"You okay, Mamí?" I ask, but she doesn't hear me.

It was so long ago that Mamí sat on Papí's lap as he played

dominoes in the backyard. It was so long ago that I heard Papí's deep voice whisper goodnight to me and tell me I could sleep safe and sound and not worry about anything because Papí was right there.

A year may seem like nothing to some people. A piece of cake. A little, cool breeze. But a year of missing Papí seems like forever to me. And it probably seems even longer to Mamí, even though she never complains. The truth is that Mamí never truly sees me until Papí comes back home. Her eyes are always far away, focused on someone or something in the future.

"I love you, Elizabeth," Mamí says, just as the plane touches its fat black wheels to the ground. And I know that I was right. For a whole year, Mamí never said that to me.

"I love you too, Mamí." Then we are both staring hard at the big double doors where Papí will soon walk through.

"There he is, Elizabeth, isn't he bonito?" Mamí's face is like a star as she waits for Papí to see her.

And then he is there in front of us, my sweet-smelling Papí, my handsome, spin-me-around Papí, and I can't breath as the world goes by faster and faster and my yellow dress spreads out like butterfly wings in the breeze.

"Oh Papí," I cry, and I feel tears on my face and I hide them in Papí's black jacket and they drip onto his polished black shoes making pin marks of happy-sadness at his feet.

And now its Mamí's turn and I see Mamí's face buried in the other side of Papí's jacket, and his other shoe has even more pin marks of water. "Oh Danielo," she cries like her heart that was broken is slowly mending.

"My beautiful muchachas, don't cry," says Papí, in a voice that is choked up tight. We cling to each other in a little circle, me, Mamí and Papí, a rock in a river of excited passengers dragging wheeled bags and shouting to relatives flowing around us.

Finally, I pull away. Mamí and Papí give me two watery smiles.

"It's time for my mermaid song," I say, clapping my hands and rubbing my eyes from all those messy tears.

"Right here?" Mamí asks, handing me a tissue.

Papí squeezes her shoulder and they lean into each other the way coconut trees do during a storm. They stare at me waiting and I feel stretched out like a dough being rolled for empanadas. I am filled with a feeling I cannot describe, and it makes me want to cry again, because Mamí's eyes are shiny black marbles and Papí's white shirt is mascara-smudged and my parents can't stop touching each other. Still, they stare at me, waiting to hear my song.

I put my hands behind my back and start singing in a sea-weedy voice. My words are soaked in salt from my tears, "The Song of a Mermaid."

Silent as a whisper
through the deep
placid sea I dream
gentle waves awake
greet my sleepy eyes.
Sing my mermaid song
to the lads and lasses
that flock to the shore.
Splash in the briny sea
greet my song
with eternity.
wander not I go no more
wander not I go no more

My song finishes, and Papí and Mamí clap softly and politely, so I look closely to see if they understand the meaning of my song. Don't go away no more, Papí. Don't go away. But they are already grabbing Papí's luggage and walking towards the truck.

"Ven acá, Elizabeth," Mamí turns to me in mid-step, and her voice smiles with her words, so different from her usual abrupt command.

"I'm right here," I whisper, trailing behind them. I walk on my tippy toes, humming the last lines of my mermaid song to myself.

"Wander not I go no more/wander not I go no more." I do my best to swallow the feeling that something's not right.

3

brandt
FIRE, FIRE BURNING BRIGHT

JARED HAS ADHD. He has to see a psychiatrist once a month and he takes a white pill every day that is not a vitamin. Mommy does not give him the pill on weekends. On the weekends, my brother is a whole lot more fun. He talks a lot, laughs and giggles and snorts straws out his nose. He tells me about everything — black holes in space, starfish, tigers in India, and why we can't grow lemons in our New York City apartment. On Sundays, he is an altar boy at St. Anthony's church near our home. Mommy calls it his "supreme responsibility".

Jared hates it. He hates the long white robe he has to wear over his regular clothes. He hates sitting quietly next to the priest near the altar especially when I make faces at him from our front pew and he can't make any back at me. Most of all, he hates the big candles on the communion table that he has to light with a long, waxy thing called a taper.

"Something's not right." Jared tells me when we are getting dressed for church. It's the Sunday before school starts. I'm struggling to tie my shoelaces, which have knotted up all by themselves in the closet since last week Sunday.

"Like what?" I ask.

"I don't know." He shrugs and bends down. In one quick yank, he untangles my knots. "It's those candles."

"Boys are you ready?" Mommy shouts from the living room.

"Are you afraid you'll burn yourself?" I ask him.

He frowns at the wall. His voice is low so Mommy doesn't hear us. "Maybe."

Before we leave the apartment, Mommy tells Jared the same thing she does every single Sunday, "Being an altar boy is a big honour, Jared. I hope you realize how important this supreme responsibility is."

Jared doesn't answer.

"You hearing me?" asks Mommy.

"Yes, of course I'm hearing you. I'm right here."

"Don't be rude, mister. We're going to church. Try to act like it."

Mommy hasn't figured out that being quiet is Jared's way of not being rude. He really wants to say something like, "If it's so important, why don't you do it." But he doesn't.

On this Sunday before school starts, Mass is about 'New Beginnings'. There are wall hangings with the words in bright bold colours. Jared leaves us at the church door to put on his hated robe. When Mass starts, he's slumping in his seat next to the priest. I wiggle my eyebrows at him like, "What's up?" He leans back in his velvet chair and gives me a blank stare.

Mommy frowns at her hymn book, and when the singing begins I sing as loudly as I can because that is my favourite part of Mass. Then, it's time for the sermon. Father Eugene gets up by the pulpit and begins his big talk. I listen because most times he tells us a nice story and I love stories as much as I love singing.

Today, Father Eugene starts off with, "God has a plan for

each of us. A special plan for Your life." He looks right at me and I sit up tall. I wonder what my plan is and I forget about Jared.

"But how do we know what our plan is?" asks Father Eugene.

"Exactly," I say. Mommy glances down at me and puts her finger to her lips.

"Have faith. God's plan for your life is waiting." Is Father Eugene staring at me? I look around and some people are nodding their heads in agreement and some are falling asleep.

I close one eye and look at Father Eugene. How long is the plan going to wait? I want to raise my hand and ask like in school but we can't do that in church although I don't see why not.

Maybe Jared will know what my plan is. He knows everything. I look around for Jared but he's not in his chair near the altar. He's not in the sanctuary by the pulpit. He's not lighting the tall communion candles. He's gone.

Father Eugene keeps talking about plans and our purpose in life. I stop listening because suddenly I see something very strange. And I smell it, too.

"Mommy," I whisper, tugging on her arm. "Do you smell the smoke?"

Mommy's busy listening to Father Eugene and shakes off my hands. "It's just the candles, honey, shush."

Smoke slips silently out from under the side door of the sanctuary. Wisps of white swirling clouds, like if you rubbed a genie bottle and a genie is getting ready to pop out. It's coming from behind the same door that Jared goes in and out of when he has to fetch the priest's robes or the taper to light the candles.

Can't Father Eugene smell the smoke? Or Mommy? And

where is Jared? I cough loudly. But no one does anything.

I cough louder as if I can't breathe, which is almost true as the smoke is starting to flow towards the front pew in a deadly snake form, weaving through the air like it wants to bite me.

Mommy turns startled eyes at me. She whips out a tissue from her purse and hands it to me. Her hands are trembling as her eyes dart all around the front of the church. "Brandt, where's your brother?"

I cover my nose and mouth with the tissue. By now even Father Eugene can see that smoke is filling up the front of the sanctuary. Voices behind us are buzzing. Everyone is murmuring and standing up. Father Eugene hasn't finished his sermon and he looks upset that the congregation is pointing at the door where the smoke is coming from and picking up their purses and hats.

No one is waiting for the priest to say "Go in peace," like he usually does at the end of church. They are rushing out of the pews and across the marble floor to the doors.

"I'm coming right back," says Mommy. She stands up quickly and her hymn book hits the floor in a loud Whap! She rushes up to the pulpit, which is not allowed, but Mommy doesn't seem to care.

"My son is back there." I hear her shouting to Father Eugene. She points to the door where the smoke is escaping faster and faster changing from a snake into a dragon now.

Father Eugene shakes his head at her, but Mommy has her own plan. As the church-goers continue to file out the back doors, Mommy pushes through the smoky door, holding her lace scarf across her nose and eyes like one of those movie bandits who rob trains. She looks just like Butch Cassidy or The Sundance Kid, who are Jared's favourite movie heroes because, like he told me once, they don't care about rules.

I watch her disappear behind the white cloud. I cover my nose with my shirt sleeve because the smoke is getting in my throat and eyes. Father Eugene comes down from his pulpit, grabs my hand and pulls me along to the back doors.

"Wait," I tell him.

"We'll wait outside," he says and grips my hand harder and pulls me through the huge wooden doors outside into the fresh air. The screeching sound of fire engines gets closer and closer. I look around for Mommy and Jared and my heart beats as loudly as the sirens.

When Father Eugene lets go of my hand I hurry to the side door of the church. I slip inside and immediately I taste the bitter scorching of smoke in my throat. I dip two fingers into the fountain of holy water and make the sign of the cross on my chest. The water feels so cool that I stick my entire hand in and scoop up as much holy water as I can and splash it on my face. The holy trinity drips down my church shirt, and makes dark spots on my Sunday shoes.

I kneel down and look toward the front altar that is now completely covered in smoke. Where's Mommy? Where's Jared? I can't see anything, not even the big wooden crucifix on the wall behind the altar. The smell of smoke is so bad I hold my breath and I feel dizzy and cold even though it's very hot. I remember what they told us in school in case of a fire. I lay down on the marble floor but the air around me gets hotter and hotter like

I'm in an oven.

"Bubba!" I hear a voice. "Bubba, where are you?"

It's Jared. He's the only one who calls me Bubba.

"Here," I try to shout back but I'm choking on smoke.

I hear bumps and cursing then someone grabs my arm. I can't see him through the smoke but I know that grip anywhere. It's strong and impatient. Jared yanks my arm really hard, like I'm a knot and he is trying to undo me. He pushes open the side door with his other hand, dragging me behind him. We reach the green bushes at the side of the church and the sirens are right in my ears. I'm still coughing and choking on the smoke.

"What were you doing, stupid?"

"Looking for you," I splutter.

Jared shakes his head. "That was dumb, Bubba, when you see smoke you run the other way."

A firefighter in a bright red coat swoops me up in his arms and tells Jared to hurry up and follow him. "Good work, son," he tells Jared when we reach the sidewalk across the street from the church. Mommy runs up crying and thanking the firefighter.

The firefighter nods at Jared, "Thank him, he saved your son."

Mommy looks at Jared and cries even more. Then she hugs me, and then Jared, then me again, and she even tries to hug the firefighter but he has work to do and he leaves.

Father Eugene comes over. "I'm so sorry," he says. But he doesn't look sorry.

"How did this happen?" Mommy asks, and we all look at Jared.

He doesn't say anything. Father Eugene doesn't say anything.

No one says anything at all. I wait to hear Mommy accuse Jared. Or for Father Eugene to get mad at him. But he doesn't.

Mommy is busy wiping her eyes when a firefighter stalks out of the side church door and right up to Father Eugene. He's holding the long taper thing in his hand. At that moment I see Father Eugene's face change from the one in charge to the one in trouble. I'd know that "Oh no!" look anywhere.

"There's petrol on this wick," the firefighter says. "Petrol!"

We all look at Father Eugene. He bites his lips. "It makes it easier to light the tall candles," he says.

"You put petrol on the taper and then give it to a child to light? Are you crazy?"

I don't think Jared likes being called a child. He's thirteen. I don't think Father Eugene likes being asked if he's crazy either. His eyes bug out at the firefighter.

Mommy snaps into her lawyer mode and her grey eyes are like bullets aimed at poor Father Eugene who has no idea how mad she can get.

Before Mommy can say a word, the firefighter tells Father Eugene to come with him to fill out a report. Father Eugene says he's sorry about ten more times as he walks away.

Then, it's just me, Mommy and Jared standing together on the sidewalk as the firefighters open the church doors wide, usher people far away and do their smoke-clearing jobs.

I look at my brother. His face is covered with black smudges, and his long white robe is dirty and ripped. Jared looks at me. "You look like you played in a tar puddle," he says.

"Same as you," I retort, and we both grin at the exact same

time. Which almost never happens!

Later that day after long baths, calls from Daddy to make sure we're okay, and an early dinner, Mommy tells Jared that he doesn't have to be an altar person anymore.

Jared looks like she just gave him a present. His smile has all three of his dimples, which we never usually see.

"Was Jared fired?" I ask.

"Was I fired?" Jared makes a loud hooting noise. "I hope that was a pun, Bubba." Mommy laughs along with Jared, which makes me happy, but I have no idea what's so funny.

"What's a pun?" I ask. But they're too busy laughing to tell me.

Mommy stops laughing first and gets serious. "It wasn't funny, though," she says. "You could've been seriously hurt."

Jared stops laughing. I remember how Mommy went rushing through that smoky door to find Jared. Jared must be remembering it, too, because he says softly, "So could you, Mommy."

The kitchen clock ticks loudly in the silence that follows. Sometimes, silence is what you need to let love find you. Because in that silent space Mommy reaches out her arms and Jared slips into them.

4

elizabeth
ONLY ONE WISH

APÍ'S VACATION IS LIKE A PARTY every day. Doña Maria has packed her cupboards with lots of food and the fridge with bottles of beer for Papí's visit. Mamí will cook feasts of roasted pig, and sancocho stew, and Papí will play dominoes in the yard with Jose, and with Tío Franco, Mamí's and Doña Maria's brother who brings his crazy laughter to our house.

On his first day home, while Mamí and Doña Maria cook the first of many feasts to come, Papí walks around the town saying hello to everyone he meets. I walk alongside holding his hand and waiting patiently for him to say Hola and have a welcome home drink or snack at every restaurant and bar we pass. Sosúa has restaurants and bars at every corner and some in between, so this welcome home trip takes all afternoon. I don't care though because I'm with Papí. I squeeze his fingers as we walk just to make sure it's really him and not a dream.

When we reach Sosúa beach, I say, "We can take a quick welcome home dip!" I'm teasing because Papí is still in his travelling pants and shoes and I'm still wearing my brand new yellow dress. But I would jump in if he said yes.

Papí frowns. "No, hija. Plenty time to go swimming. Plenty time to play games."

It's my turn to frown. "Two weeks is not plenty time."

We continue walking past the beach vendors selling cut-open coconuts with piña colada drinks for the tourists, past the cigar man selling expensive Dominican cigars for the rich Dominicanos from Santo Domingo who come up on long weekends, and past the souvenir shops selling ceramic dolls and canvases of colourful beach scenes for foreigners to take home a piece of our country.

Finally, Papí and I turn toward home. Papí says very gently, "Elizabeth, we don't have to be in the same place to be close. We'll always be together. You and your Mamí are always right here with me." He points to his heart and his head. "Do you understand? Now, let's go see what your mother has cooked for us."

I walk silently beside him thinking of his words as we twist and turn through the streets that lead to Doña Maria's green house near the rocky sea cliffs.

"Do you think you knew me in my other life?" I ask Papí.

Papí stops short. "Another life? What other life?"

"Before I was me." I stop in mid-step. "Tío Franco says I used to be a mermaid in another life? Because I love the sea so much. What do you think you were in your other life?"

Papí and I start walking again. He's thinking about my question because his lips are puckered and he's staring into space instead of looking at where we're going.

"Elizabeth," he says seriously as the green house looms up ahead. "I don't think I had another life. I'm just me. Your Papí."

"But what if you die, you'll have another life, so what do you think you'll be. Or what would you like to be?"

Papí's eyes are twitching around looking for a good answer. "Who says I'm dying?"

"I said, 'what if'. And you're supposed to say what you feel in your heart. Not think about it."

"Well in that case, if I die I want to come back as your Papí. Again."

"Really?"

"Si," he says. "Is that okay?" He smiles a tender kind of smile at me that I've missed for a year or more.

I smile back at my tall, handsome father. "Okay," I say. "That's okay with me."

Papí wipes his brow like he was sweating. "Thank goodness you'll take me back!"

We laugh and laugh like it was the funniest thing and we reach home arm in arm to find Mamí has set the outdoor table with dishes of food and a jug of lemonade and an ice bucket full of beer and wine and a big chocolate cake in the middle.

I run inside and grab a candle to stick in the middle of the cake.

"It's not anyone's birthday," says Mamí as she puts down another heavy bowl of food. She says that every time I put a candle in a cake that she bakes for us.

"It's to make a wish." I say this every time, too.

Mamí's turn to say, "Wishes don't grow on trees, mi hija. We should not waste them."

Papí interrupts. "Let her make as many wishes as she wants." He knows I love to blow out candles for any reason or no reason at all.

Mamí frowns, maybe because Papí is messing up our little routine which always ends with Mamí giving in and me kissing her. Or maybe because Mamí doesn't like that Papí is on my side. Or maybe, and this is what I think, it's because Papí has made wishes seem so ordinary. Like they are everywhere. Mamí and I both know that there is only one wish worth wishing for and he's standing right there in front of us.

Papí can tell he has messed up, and he steps backwards. Mamí rushes toward him, "It's okay, she makes wishes all the time. Most of them are for you to come home soon."

"Well, this time I'm wishing you won't leave." I say it defiantly, and it's how I feel. I'll fight to keep my wish.

Mamí looks at me in shock. Papí shakes his head in defeat. "She doesn't understand," he says to Mamí. "I have to work there."

Mamí shushes him with a kiss on both cheeks then one on his forehead and a last one on his lips. There are no kisses for me. Papí hugs her tightly and they stand under the yellow tree snuggled close, leaving me out.

"I do understand." I mutter fiercely. But they don't hear me or maybe, they just don't want to.

Later that evening, after we eat all the food and Papí and Jose and Tío Franco drink the beers and Doña Maria has poured glasses of wine for her and Mamí, they open up the dominos table under the tree and Papí sits in his favourite chair. Mamí perches like a bird on his lap.

I say goodnight and go to bed, but I watch them from my window. Tío Franco is the only one who sees me, and he smiles in my direction, but soon, he too gets caught up in the dominoes game, slapping the small ivory bars with black dots hard on the table.

Their little corner of the garden is lit up with fairy lights twined around the tree and romantic bachata music playing on the radio. In my corner, the world is dark and the only light is from the faraway stars shining like small white pebbles in the sky.

I watch as Papí leans forward in his wooden chair, one arm around Mamí, and slaps dominoes down on the table to match Tío Franco's moves. Jose slaps his own dominoes down harder than Papí's. The men laugh and gesture wildly arguing over points. Mamí grabs more bottles of beer for them and sits back on Papí's knee. Doña Maria cuts the cake, the cake I never got to make a wish on. They play and drink and eat for a long time and no one looks up at my window where I wait for a falling star to make my wish.

5

brandt
EVERYTHING BREAKS

ARED SAYS I'M TOO YOUNG to remember when
we lived with Daddy in a big, pink house with roses
in a garden and a garage that looked like a barn. Our
house was in Queens and it had a big front porch and a
round tower like a castle. None of the other houses on our block
looked like ours.

I might not have Jared's amazing brain, but I do remember
that Jared used to sit next to me in the back seat of Daddy's car.
I remember that Mommy's long black hair hung over the seat
in front of me and I would reach forward from my car seat to
try and touch it. Daddy drove and changed the radio stations
until he found rap music and he'd rap along with the radio while
tapping the steering wheel. After a while, Mommy would change
the station and we'd listen to salsa music. Rap and salsa, rap
and salsa, that's how it went on our long drives to upstate New
York to Bear Mountain, or to Wave Hill Park in the city. I always
remember the stations changing because Mommy and Daddy
didn't like each other's music.

They were like a see-saw, going up and down, down and up,
with me and Jared on the side watching. Every once in a while
they'd level out, balanced in the middle, teeter-tottering in that
spot where everything is perfect.

Now, Mommy, Jared, and I are trying to balance on a triangle with all three sides pointy and sharp. Mommy says her job is demanding, that Jared is challenging, that New York is dangerous, and that she will never find her soul mate in this rough and tumble city. I hear her talking to Alex her best friend who is a girl with a boy's name. She's a lawyer like Mommy. I like her because she was the one who nick-named Jared, the "Amazing Brain."

She loves Jared even though everyone else calls him "difficult". She says Jared is sensitive and has to put up strong defenses to block his heart from breaking every day. I am listening to Alex and Mommy talk one night as they sit at our kitchen table. Mommy wants to send Jared away to a strict school, a military place, she says.

"Are you crazy, Izzy, you'll kill that sensitive boy."

`I hold my breath. Alex is right. Mommy can't do that. I won't let her.

"I just want what's best for him. I want him to be happy. He always looks miserable."

Alex snorts and I giggle in my hiding spot under the table.

"Maybe you're the one who's unhappy. That boy is fine. Just leave him alone."

"I think sometimes he hates me."

"Oh, stop feeling sorry for yourself, Izzy."

I feel the table wobble as someone stands up to get something from the fridge.

"Alex, I'm serious, he hates me because of the divorce. He won't forgive me ever, that's how I feel."

Big sigh from Alex. "Stop it, Izzy. Things break all the time.

Hearts break but get mended. Families break apart and form new families. Everything breaks. That's how new things can start."

Alex speaks in what I think must be her lawyer voice. It's serious and no-nonsense. A little bit sad, too.

"Exactly!" I want to shout out but I press my lips together.

"So we can't even count on family? That's what you're saying?"

"No. I'm not saying that. But there's all kinds of families. Anyone who is connected to you by heart and soul is your family, too.

"I like that," said Mommy.

I did too, but I couldn't speak up.

Alex laughed. "Yep. You have your family you're born into and the tribe you create yourself."

"What about the people who are in both?"

"Well, that's perfection." Alex said, sounding like she'd just scored a run. I almost bounded out from under the table then but I stayed quiet.

When Alex left that day I thought about what she'd said. I took out a piece of paper and drew two big circles. In one circle I wrote "Tribe" and in the other circle I penned, "Family."

"What're you doing, Bubba?" Jared was standing over my shoulder staring down with a smirk on his face.

"I'm writing down everyone who is in my Tribe and in my Family."

"You're so weird."

I looked at Jared out of half-closed eyes. I sat back in my chair and stared at his name in my Tribe Circle and in my Family Circle. It was the first name I'd written. And it was in both places.

"Okay," I muttered. I began erasing his name from my Tribe circle.

"Why're you erasing me?"

"Cause everything breaks."

Jared shook his head. "Really weird."

He turned to walk out the room but then he doubled back. He took the pen out of my hand and scribbled his name back in my Tribe circle in really big letters. "Don't erase me again, Bubba or I'll beat you up."

I laughed. It was just like I knew. Maybe everything breaks. Toys, computer games, bicycle tires, cars. But not me and Jared.

6

elizabeth
TRAPPED IN A BOX

SCHOOL STARTS JUST A FEW days before Papí is ready to return to Neuva York. He and Mamí meet my new teacher, Señora Martinez, and Papí makes Señora Martinez promise that she'll make me work hard so I can get into a private high school that he will pay for from all the money he earns in Neuva York.

Señora Martinez smiles and nods. "Claro que si." I can tell she is impressed by Papí.

I think my education is just fine in the school I'm in. But I keep my mouth shut. To me it seems as if Papí and Mamí are inventing reasons for him to go back. Well, Papí is anyway. Mamí just says yes and agrees. At least my best friend Clara is in my class and when I tell her how I feel about Papí going back to the United States, she understands. "That really sucks a big mango," she says and we laugh, but my laugh is a dead sound.

The night before Papí leaves for Neuva York, I wake up with a throbbing headache and I'm vomiting and crying. Mamí holds my head and asks me over and over what's wrong. Is it your head? Your stomach? No, I want to shout, it's my heart. Because honestly, what's wrong is that my heart feels like it's expanding then collapsing, expanding then collapsing like a star that is too bright and will explode any minute.

The next morning, the clouds are crying and a mist clings

to the top of Mt. Isabel. I drop my glass of orange juice and the pieces fly to all corners of the room while the yellow liquid seeps into the wooden floor slats. Mamí, who is rushing about the kitchen mashing plantains and chopping red onions for mofongo, Papí's special goodbye meal, drops her knife and shakes her head at me.

"Not today, Elizabeth," she cries.

"Sorry," I mumble as I drag the mop across the floor.

"Put on your slippers!" Mamí's anger is lifting the roof off its hinges. "You'll cut yourself."

I look over at Papí sitting at the table in his black suit and shiny shoes. His hands are steepled on the table and he looks far away from here as if the problems of broken glass and spilled juice are not a part of his life. Not anymore. Even his suitcase leans against the door half in, half out like it's already on its way to New York.

I finish cleaning the floor and sit down next to Papí at our little kitchen table. I don't say anything. I don't look at him. I trace the flower design on my new glass of orange juice with my finger and try to remember him saying that we are close even if we aren't in the same country.

"Mi amor," Papí says, reaching over and taking my hand. "I'll call you every week and we'll talk about school and your friends, and your . . . mermaids." He's trying to make me smile, but it doesn't work. For the first time I don't care about mermaids. "Something's not right. I don't want you to go, Papí." I sound like a broken record. Or a parrot.

Mamí groans. "Not that again, Elizabeth. If you're going to spoil your Papí's last day, then please go back to your room."

I start to cry at Mamí's harsh words, at Papí's unseeing eyes, at the mist and the dark clouds. Everything feels on the verge of breaking. Like my juice glass.

No one says a word. Papí eats the mofongo, but leaves most of his food on the plate. Jose arrives with the truck and hoists Papí's suitcase onto his shoulders. He looks sad at his friend's departure. At least he shows his real feelings, not like Mamí who has a plastic flower in her hair and a plastic smile sliding across her lips.

Then, quickly, before I can decide if to eat, or say I'm sorry, or protest again, it's all hugs, kisses, and last words, and Papí is sitting in the truck next to Jose. I run up to the passenger side and press my hand into Papí's and whisper, "Come back, soon Papí."

Papí wipes his eyes and nods firmly. "It's a promise."

Mamí is crying like there's no tomorrow. Gone are her plastic smiles. Black tears trickle down her cheeks and she can't wipe them fast enough so she gives up. Doña Maria comes down from her side of the big, green casa and puts an arm around Mamí's shoulders. "He'll be back before we know it." But her words are grains of sand blowing in our face.

That night, after we get a call from Papí saying he arrived safely in New York, I start having my dreams. I dream I'm trapped in a box and I can't breathe. I wake up coughing and smelling smoke.

After three nights of the same nightmare, I tell Clara about it.

"Ewww, that's really gross. Or crazy." She assesses me for the crazy factor. "Probably crazy." Clara is no-nonsense. She is better at maths and science than me and loves to solve problems.

My dream becomes a problem for her to solve. Clara begins drawing pictures of small, dark boxes on loose leaf paper and asking if any of them look familiar.

"No!" I tell her over and over again. Because they don't. My box is full of light. Yet it's stifling me. It's huge, but small, too. It's scary, but beautiful. It's upside down. My box ripples and spins and presses me so flat I'm almost invisible. My box feels like it will cave in on me if I breathe too much so I hold my breath.

I try to tell Doña Maria about my dream but she insists on a drink of nutmeg and aloe to clean me out. I tell Mamí about my dream and she says it's my imagination working too hard and I must stop thinking so much and be normal.

Normal?

I tell Clara I need to be normal and she says normal sucks mangoes and I laugh.

Every morning when I arrive in class late because I overslept because of my dream, Clara looks at me with a question in her eyes, like, "Again?"

She doesn't have to say it out loud. We've been best friends for years now and I can read her mind. Like she can read mine.

I nod my head. "Yes, again."

She starts a new series of drawings to help figure it out. What I don't tell her is that the feeling of being trapped is getting stronger. It's yanking off my covers and whispering in my ears. And the smell of smoke lingers even after I wake up.

7

brandt
THE STORY OF EVERYTHING

SECOND GRADE IS ALL ABOUT homework and pink detention slips for not doing it. There's no more afternoon snacks, no more colouring of large posters to pin on the boards, and no more story time.

I ask Jared, "Do we ever get story time back?"

He shakes his head. "Nope, Bubba, from here on stories are zilch." He pretends he's cutting his throat with his finger. I would laugh except for the no more story time which is like hearing you can't ever have ice-cream again.

On the weekend after school has started, Mommy is busy preparing for a trial and we have to be really quiet or else. "Read your brother a story," Mommy says, closing our door and putting a finger to her lips.

Jared rolls his eyes. "He can read his own story." He tosses Robin Hood on my bed. Not the thick one with page after page of black words and no drawings. But the large picture book Robin Hood where a happy guy is prancing along on horse back with a brown sack on his shoulder. All of the words are bubbles coming out of the people's mouths.

I settle down on my bed and flip the pages. I glance over at Jared to see if he'll change his mind and read me the story, but he's reading his own book. After I have flipped the pages a bunch of times I let out a big sigh. Jared makes a bubbling sound with his mouth and ignores me. I go to our bookshelf and search around for another book to read. After taking one book down, then another and another, Jared looks over and says, "What exactly are you looking for? You don't even read."

"I would if it was the right story."

Jared makes a loud hrrumph sound in his throat and goes back to his book.

I sit on our floor surrounded by a heap of books. Jared says, "So, what exactly is the right story?"

"I don't know."

"That helps," says Jared, shaking his head.

"A story about everything," I tell him.

"No story is about everything."

"Well, that's the one I want to read."

"Well then Bubba, you'll have to write it yourself."

"Maybe I will."

Jared and I laugh even though I'm kind of serious. We laugh so hard that Mommy pushes open our door and tells us we're being too noisy.

"And why are all those books on the floor?"

Jared smirks. "Brandt's going to write a story."

Mommy's face lights up. "That's wonderful, Brandt."

"Ask him what it'll be about," adds Jared.

Mommy looks from Jared to me. She waits with her hand on the door knob. "Well?"

"Everything."

Mommy stares at me for a long silent minute. Like she has no idea what to say. Finally she speaks. "Okay, sounds good." Then she and Jared look at each other and they both smile as if it's a joke. Which it isn't.

"Are we going to be in this story of everything, Brandt honey?" asks Mommy.

"Of course."

"Is Batman going to be in it, too?" Jared asks.

I nod.

"What about my island, the Dominican Republic?" asks Mommy.

"Yes," I tell them.

"What else?" asks Jared. "The sea, the beach, mermaids?"

"Yup. I said everything!" For the first time ever I feel as if Jared and Mommy are on the same side of the fence and I am on the other and in a way I don't mind.

Jared laughs and Mommy looks like she wants to but she presses her smile down and asks, "Will your Daddy and school and your teachers and church all be in it?"

"Of course. And the Twin Towers and Mr. Hernandez and the yellow balloon I saw that day at lunch."

"What about Grand Pop?" ask Mommy, talking about her father who lives in the D.R. and calls us every week.

"Yes, he'll definitely be in the story," I say.

"Will there be food in this story of everything?" asks Jared.

"Yes, especially yummy desserts!" I say.

"Dogs, cats, ponies?" asks Mommy.

"Yes, and even horses. Like in Robin Hood."

"Great," says Mommy, sitting on the edge of Jared's bed as if she's forgotten her trial.

"One last question," Jared says. "Will there be any girls in it?" He wiggles his eyebrows at me and I burst out laughing again.

"Maybe," I say. "A nice one, who likes you," I smirk back at Jared.

"Ewwww!" Jared says and Mommy laughs and we continue talking about all the things that will be in my Story of Everything.

"Okay," Mommy says after a nice long time. "I have to get back to work. But is this going to be a happy story or a sad one? I hope it's happy."

I shake my head. "It'll be happy and sad. It's about everything."

8

elizabeth
IT'S TOO LATE

FEW WEEKS AFTER SCHOOL has started, Señor Oliver, our school principal, comes to the door of the classroom looking like he is going to faint. He speaks rapidly to Señora Martinez, who drops her chalk and reaches behind her for her desk as if she will sink through the floor without its support. I have never seen that expression on anyone's face before. Señora Martinez looks as if the she has been stabbed right in her heart. It is scary enough without her turning to look right at me.

"Elizabeth," she says in a shaky voice.

That's when I know.

And so does Clara. She reaches over and grabs my hand and all those boxes Clara has drawn over the past few weeks come closing down around me. I'm sinking into the paper, into the desk, into the floor and I really don't want to hear whatever Señora Martinez is going to tell me.

I yank my hand from Clara's grasp and begin to hum. I hum and hum getting louder and louder and I cover my ears with my hands as Señora Martinez walks toward me. For one crazy moment I want to push her away to see if she will spin around in a circle.

As she gets closer, I pick up my history book and bury my head in it, reading slowly, pronouncing the words aloud, one by one like the teacher has just asked me to recite the history lesson for the class.

"Elizabeth," Señora Martinez says again, speaking softly.

I ignore her and continue to read out loud. The closer she comes, the louder I read. I'll drown her out. I'll read so loudly she won't be able to tell me whatever it is that the principal just told her. Whatever it is that is going to change my life right here in front of the entire seventh grade class.

But neither my words nor my fears put a stop to Señora Martinez and there she is standing above my desk. The mountain came to me. She touches my arm, and strokes my hair, and pulls the book gently away from my arms.

Clara begins to cry. Why is she crying? But then I hear the sobs in my own throat and I bury my face in my hands. It's true. The boxes are true. I can't breathe. I'm choking and I can hardly breathe.

"Come with me, Elizabeth," says Señora Martinez.

I pack up my books, counting them as I slip them one by one into my school bag. I gather up my pencils and pens and put them into my bag. I refuse to look at Señora Martinez again but I hear her crying now. How dare she cry? How dare she act like this thing, whatever it is, has happened to her?

I don't know why I'm angry at her, but I am. The entire class is watching me be punished and I didn't do anything wrong.

"Are you ready?" Señora Martinez asks in a choked up voice.

I shake my head no. I open my desk top higher and begin to take out every single thing inside, as if I'm packing up never to return.

Clara comes over to my desk without asking permission to get up in class. She helps me gather every single pencil and eraser bits, and pieces of notebook paper and even empty gum wrappers. We stuff them all into my bulging backpack while Señora Martinez waits patiently. The class is more silent than I ever knew it could be.

Then Clara gives me a hug and I hug her back and I turn to follow Señora Martinez out of the classroom like I'm headed to war. My bag hangs heavily on my shoulder as I march down the hall with Señora Martinez's tear-streaked face beside me.

In the hallway, teachers are exclaiming and covering their mouths with hands. Some have tears on their faces. The principal is pacing up and down by the front door to the school. Señora Martinez puts her hand against my back and I'm not sure if she is pushing me forward or trying to hold me back. I almost want to turn and cry in her dress but I keep walking toward the doors.

That's when I see Jose, Doña Maria's chofer, pull up in the truck outside. Principal Oliver goes outside to talk to him and I stand on the threshold between the cool hallway and the hot sunshine of a world that has forever changed in a way I don't know, but somehow I do know. After a few moments, the principal comes over to me and says in a voice trying hard to be steady, "Cuídate, Elizabeth."

It's too late to take care, I think, but I nod and walk silently to the truck and climb in. Jose does not even try to disguise his tears. He is crying openly and a horrible numbness starts in my fingers and crawls up my arms and neck.

"Is it Mamí?" I ask.

Jose shakes his head no. But I know that already. I already know that it isn't Mamí.

I lean back against the seat for the short drive home. I clutch the straps of my backpack sitting on my lap. All of Sosúa's boisterous noises have ceased. The motoconchos are parked haphazardly along the curbs while their drivers huddle outside the restaurants and bars talking, gesturing, and peering up at television screens that seem to blare loud enough for the fish at the bottom of the sea to hear. As we drive slowly past the open bars I see images on the television screens, like a movie. Fire and flames, tall buildings engulfed by smoke. My heart shudders. I can smell the smoke through the tiny television boxes. Suddenly, I know exactly what the box was and I wish I could tell Clara to stop drawing because now we have our answer.

9

brandt
IN THE BEGINNING ...

Y MOTHER SAYS SHE KNOWS exactly who loves her and can place them in numerical order as to how much they love her. On September 11, I have just started second grade and already I miss my first grade teacher, Ms. Simon, who never shouted, never banged her hand on a table and never made me cry - all acts of terror my new teacher, Ms. Feliciano, has committed in the first week of school.

Every day after school, Jared and I wait for Mommy to come home from work. On September 11, we go home early. Jared picks me up from my new classroom and holds my hand all the way home. Jared never holds my hand. Jared doesn't talk to me at all. He doesn't turn on the computer. He doesn't let me turn on the television. He doesn't do anything but lie on his bottom bunk bed and stare up at the top bunk. When I try to turn on the computer, he shouts at me, "Turn it off."

"Why?" I ask.

"Mom might call," is all he says.

Jared never cared about Mommy calling before. It is a constant fight they have. She complains that he's always on the internet so she cannot get through on the telephone. She asks him to at least wait until she calls to see if we are alright and then he can go on the internet. Jared never listens.

"It's important," she tells him, her voice rising when he

shrugs his shoulders at her. Her face gets red and she takes deep breaths and then goes to her bedroom and closes the door.

But on September 11, Jared doesn't turn on the internet to check out his newest Neopet. I sit on the floor next to our bunk beds. I look at Jared and he turns away so I can't see his face. Something weird is happening. At school, the teachers had been scurrying in the hallways and lining us up to leave a half-day early. Ms. Feliciano had been extra nice and had asked the class if any of us had parents who worked in or near the World Trade Center.

I raised my hand proudly because my mother worked right there. I said that she was a lawyer in a big company and I had visited the tall towers and ridden the elevator up those bridges to the sky many times. Then, I saw the look on Ms. Feliciano's face. Why was she scrunching up her eyes and frowning? I said my mother worked there - wasn't that the right answer? She came over and patted my head and then left the room. When she came back, Jared was with her. He's in the eighth grade. He's been diagnosed a genius and got to skip third grade. I wished I could skip second grade. But I haven't been diagnosed anything as yet. Jared told me quietly to get my back pack and come on.

Now, here we are – waiting for something. At least, Jared is waiting for something, so I wait, too.

Except pretty soon, my stomach starts growling and I go into the kitchen to make a peanut butter and grapes sandwich. Jared doesn't say a word when I smash the grapes between my bread. Usually, he says it's gross. I say it's the same thing as putting grape jelly on bread. I just skip the jelly part and go straight for the grapes. He says it's a baby thing to do. I hate it when he calls me a baby. But I get him back. I tell him I am Mommy's joy. That's what she calls me, her joy.

But then Jared always snaps back, "You might be her joy, but I'm her heart."

He's right. Mommy calls Jared her 'heart' and she calls me her 'joy'. I'm not sure which is better. Heart or Joy? I mean, you love with your heart, so she really loves Jared. But you're happy if you feel joy so I make her happy. But not everything you love makes you happy. Sometimes, the person you love the most makes you the saddest. Life is funny and I have a lot to figure out and all this waiting for something to happen is making me hungry, so I eat.

10

elizabeth

THE WORLD IS CRAZY

OSE DRIVES ONWARD not stopping to buy his usual numbers ticket, which he swears will win him a million pesos one day. Up ahead, past the synagogue built by the Jewish settlers who came to Sosúa many years ago, past the cheese factory which they founded as a business enterprise, and past the barracks where they first lived together as refugees from Hitler's regime, is Doña Maria's green house. I can already see the clouds hanging over the house like crying angels. Whatever has happened it is not something small. Not something easy. Not something that can be fixed.

The house stands alone next to the sea, overshadowed by a hill of many names. The house was built by her captain husband, the oldest son of a white Spanish clan who defied his family by marrying Maria, a poor, dark-skinned campesino. I think about all these things as we drive slowly through the roads.

I think about Mamí growing up with her strict father, Alejandro. He was a farmer who grew plantains and yams in Moca and worked all day and drank all night. That's what I heard Tío Franco say. Dona Maria is Mamí's and Tío's much older half-sister. Dona Maria worked in Sosúa and sent money home to help raise her little sister and brother until the day she ran off with the sea captain. Abuelo never forgave her for not getting married in the famous Moca Cathedral and he still does not speak to her.

When Doña Maria's husband died, Abuelo spat on his grave and said, "Púdrete en el infierno." Even though I was only seven-years-old at the time, I already knew that was the worse thing you could whisper to a dead person.

Mamí tried to make it up to Doña Maria by going to live with her in Sosúa and helping her out in the house. After two years, Mamí sent for me and I left Moca, too, hoping my abuelo wasn't whispering anything bad as the wheels of the car taking me to a new life skidded away in the dust.

Now, as Jose drives up to the house I can see Mamí sitting on a porch rocker with her face in her hands. Doña Maria is standing over her sister stroking her hair. Mamí looks like a small child and Doña Maria looks angry. Or upset. I have never seen Doña Maria looking anything but sad so the expression on her face and the way she is standing, with her legs apart and her mouth in a thin, tight line makes me understand more than anything else that has happened so far that my entire world has changed forever.

"Come, Elizabeth," says Jose, reaching over to open the door for me. He wipes his eyes with the back of his hand. "It's a tragedy," he says, shaking his head. "A real tragedy."

I could ask Jose what is going on, but I don't want to. My heart feels like it's being pulled right out of my chest as I walk up the steps of the house, leaving my backpack on the ground. The sea is flat and still in the distance and I hear the echo of Mamí's crying through the soles of my feet.

"Papí?" I say to Doña Maria in a voice that sounds like it's coming from a tight space.

Mamí lets out a loud wail. Doña Maria nods like a paper doll who has no control over her head.

"Neuva York?"

Doña Maria nods again, her shoulders sagging this time.

My body begins to tremble all over. My hand shakes as I grab the porch railing to pull myself up the last few steps. "What happened?" I whisper. The air seems to be moving really fast or really slowly. My head gets light and I might faint or fall down but I keep a grip on the railing. My tongue gets heavy in my mouth and I'm not sure I can say another word.

"A plane crash," says Doña Maria. "Two planes. They hit the building where your Papí worked."

Mamí shrieks at Doña Maria's words and I lean backwards like she just slapped me.

Nothing is making sense but I know one thing. Something terrible has happened to Papí in Neuva York. I gulp for air. I take a deep breath. Than another one. I'm trying to get air into my lungs but they seem to have stopped working. I'm choking just like in my dreams. The box is closing in around me but it's Doña Maria's arms wrapped tightly around my shoulders and pressing me close to her chest so that I can hardly breathe.

Mamí clings to the fabric of her dress and raises it up to dry her eyes that can't stop pouring out water. I reach out from under Doña Maria's strong arms to touch Mamí's hand but Mamí looks at me like she doesn't even see me. Like I'm invisible.

"Terroristas," Jose says, joining us on the porch. "I'm so sorry. So sorry, Señoras."

I hiccup and start to cry. Mamí sees me for the first time. Her water-filled eyes focus on me. "It's all your fault, muchacha," she screeches at me.

I stare into Mamí's frantic eyes. How is this my fault?

"You put a fucú on your Papí. Before he left here. You said something bad was going to happen. And it has. You killed your father!"

"Lourdes, stop!" Doña Maria's voice could cut glass.

"It's true," Mamí cries and points at me. "She knows it's true."

I look down at the painted wooden slats of the porch. Did I put a fucú on my own father? With all my bad dreams?

"Nonsense," shouts Doña Maria. "Estás loca?

Jose crosses himself and whispers, "Ay Dios mío."

Mamí is accusing me of brujería. Doña Maria is calling Mamí crazy, and Jose is taking God's name in vain. The world is going crazy. I pull away from Doña Maria's arms and run inside the house. I throw myself on my bed and grab my pillow to my chest. I stare out the window waiting for the storm that will surely come to wash all these horrible things away. I don't realize I'm biting my lip until I taste the blood on my tongue.

"She doesn't mean it, Elizabeth," says Doña Maria, coming into my room.

Yes, she does. I saw it in her eyes. But I don't say anything to Doña Maria. I push the memory of Mamí's eyes deep down into my heart where it turns sharp and icy like a needle stabbing me whenever I breathe.

"You didn't kill your Papí. That's ridiculous. We don't even know if he was in the building when it collapsed."

I look up at my brave aunt who knows all about loss and sadness. Is it Mamí's and my turn now? Is this house always going to have grief and sorrow flowing like a river through it?

Doña Maria makes me come outside to the drawing room. "You can't stay in the room by yourself right now."

The phone is ringing but no one is answering it. Jose is fiddling with the knobs on the radio. We don't have television, which is probably a good thing because I don't want to see what I'm hearing. Two planes have crashed into the World Trade Center in Neuva York, the same buildings that looked like bridges to the sky. Papí works in one of the restaurants in the towers. As the radio announcer gives us details of buildings imploding and falling down, of fires and hellish smoke engulfing the area, and of people falling out of windows from the sky, I wrap my arms around myself to stop the terrible trembling taking over my body. I'm either sitting on ice or fiery rocks. I can't tell, with the way my body is shivering and sweating at the same time.

The radio announcer's voice does not cover up Jose's soft crying or Mamí's hiccupy sobs.

"How do we know Papí is there?" I whisper.

Mamí cries out, "He called. He called to say goodbye to me. He was coughing so much he could hardly talk. He said he felt like he was in an oven and he couldn't breathe."

I hold my breath, my cheeks puffing out with the pain of squeezing in the air one last time, and holding it. I want to feel

how Papí must have felt, all choked up and unable to breathe.
I squeeze and squeeze my last remaining breath until I'm going
to burst. It's just like in my dreams. I close my eyes and start
counting down the seconds to drowning.

"What are you doing, Elizabeth?" Doña Maria shakes me hard
and I let out the breath that I am holding. But there's not enough
air in this sad, sad house to save me.

Jose is crying so hard at Mamí's words that snot is coming
out his nose. I walk outside and across the porch. I keep walking,
leaving the sound of the radio and the crying behind.

11

brandt
THERE IS SADNESS ...

OMMY DOES NOT KNOW IT, but Jared loves her best of all. I know because of him not going on the internet on September 11. Mommy cries and cries on the sofa as she listens to her cell phone messages, as if the messages starting at 8:48 a.m. that day sums up her entire life. But it's the message she didn't get that means the most.

Mommy doesn't actually have her cell phone. She lost it on September 11. It disappeared like a lot of other things that day . . . people, buildings, and the stars I used to watch at night with Mommy when we took our walk to the park, which she won't do anymore.

A week after September 11, Mommy figures out that she can check her cell phone messages from our regular home telephone. She calls the number for a phone that had been obliterated. I learned what 'obliterated' meant this week. It means completely destroyed. Like the Towers and Mommy's cell phone.

Mommy listens to her messages over and over, and then she writes them all down, every word, filling up the blank spaces around her with information to stop her tears. It doesn't work.

1. MESSAGE RECEIVED AT 8:48 A.M. Her father calling from Sosúa. "Honey, please call me and tell me you're okay. I'm looking at the News right now. A plane just crashed into your building. I remember when we went to the salsa concert under the stars

there. Please call me and let me know you're okay."

I can hear the worry even in the written message.

2. MESSAGE RECEIVED AT 8:50 A.M. Mommy's work friend Alison calling from the office. "Izzy, where are you? We've got to get out of the office now. Meet me and Phil at the elevators. Now!"

3. MESSAGE RECEIVED AT 8:53 A.M. Rudy calling from the office.

"Izzy, tell me you're at Court and not here. Something horrible has happened. We can't tell but they're saying we should stay right where we are for now. I don't think so. We're leaving. We're at the stairs by the Women's bathroom. Meet us there."

4. MESSAGE RECEIVED AT 9:05 A.M. Mommy's sister, Sonia, calling from the Republica Dominicana. "Isabella, I am praying for you. I am praying real hard. I know you are fine. I know it." Auntie Sonia lives in Samana next to the beach and fishes every day. She stands upside down on her head to pray, which she calls meditating. I imagine her standing on her head praying for Mommy.

5. MESSAGE RECEIVED AT 9:09 A.M. Rudy calling from the office. "Izzy, it's me again. This is not an accident! We're on the stairs. It's jammed. We need to get out of here now. Where are you?"

6. MESSAGE RECEIVED AT 9:16 A.M. Grand Pop calling again. "Isabella? Call me back."

7. MESSAGE RECEIVED AT 9:23 A.M. Mommy's best friend, Alex. "Isabella, I'm in Philly at a deposition and just saw the News. Please call me and let me know you didn't go to work today, or you're having a late tea at the shop on Broadway or you're in Court at trial . . . or something!"

8. MESSAGE RECEIVED AT 9:37 A.M. Tony Hernandez calling from?

"Princessa, I hope you're okay. I'm worried about you. I know you're still mad at me, but call me and let me know you're okay." Hmmmmm. Who was that? Mommy has secret friends who call her princessa?

9. MESSAGE RECEIVED AT 9:41 A.M. Mr. Sola calling from where? "Isabella, I am asking everyone from the office to call in to my cell phone or home phone as soon as they get out of the building. There are just no words for this. Good luck." Mommy's boss. He doesn't mind if I come into the office on Saturdays with Mommy to help her make copies and staple piles of papers together with Exhibit tabs. I feel something fierce and sad in his words.

10. MESSAGE RECEIVED AT 9:45 A.M. Grand Pop calling back. "Isabella, call me as soon as you can. I am waiting."

11. MESSAGE RECEIVED AT 9:48 A.M. Daddy calling from the Brooklyn Bridge on his cell phone. "Izzy, call me and let me know where you are. I'm walking over the Bridge. I'll go get the kids from school as soon as I get home." Daddy never came to the school to get us. He did not make it to his home where he lives with his new wife until the sun was almost setting. He walked the entire way in his hard, black polished shoes and his feet hurt for a long time but he said that was nothing. Nothing at all.

There were many more messages. Messages with people crying. Messages with people sounding dazed and stuttering, and not making any sense. Messages from all the people who loved Mommy. She has a list. It is numbered and she holds it close to her.

Then, one day, Mommy turns with her eyes full of tears

toward Jared and whispers, "Why didn't you call me?"

Jared stares at her.

"Why didn't you call me at work, or on my cell, or something. Were you too busy playing on the internet?"

Jared doesn't answer her. He looks back at her and she looks at him and in between them shimmers a light that wavers up and down trying to catch them both in its rays but it can't.

I watch them and I want to shout at Mommy that Jared loves her more than everyone on that list because he didn't even turn on the computer that day. Or the television. Or anything. I want to tell her that Jared had laid on his bunk bed and closed his eyes and turned his face so that I couldn't see he was crying.

That was the only day Jared hadn't called me a baby when I made my peanut butter and grapes sandwich. It was the only day he held my hand. It was the day I knew that even though he talked back to Mommy, even though she threw up her hands and yelled at him, even though they seemed as if they were two panthers looking crossways at each other, deep down they loved each other more than anyone else. Jared was Mommy's heart. But what Mommy didn't know was that she was Jared's, too.

And, in the days following September 11, I began to understand that your heart is never wrong. It is only your mind that gets confused. Your heart tells you much more than what your mind is thinking. But Mommy isn't listening to her heart. She's keeping lists and crying.

12

elizabeth
THE VANISHING POINT

P THE ROAD from Doña Maria's home, there is a high cliff. It's rocky with huge clumps of red clay and smudges of green grass, and it overlooks the sea. I like to climb up there and sit perched on one of the big boulders with my hand shielding the dazzling sun from my eyes. From this cliff I see the ships sailing far away on the rolling Atlantic Ocean, and I can imagine the mermaids swimming beneath the rocky overhang. But not today. Today I see nothing.

Blue above, blue below, and in between so much blue my eyes close down until I am squinting at the horizon where the sea and the sky are a line blended together. This is called the vanishing point. Tío Franco told me this. Whenever he draws mountains or rivers or the ocean, he looks for their vanishing point. It is where one thing disappears into another.

As I sit there all alone on the cliff, I wonder, could my Papí have disappeared into something else, blending into his own vanishing point? And if he has, how in the world was I going to live with that? And how was Mamí going to do it?

13

brandt
THEN THERE IS CHAOS ...

"UT WHY DO WE have to go?" I ask Jared.

"Because."

"Where is Sosúa?"

"Near Puerto Plata - you have already been there, you just don't remember it."

"Is it far?"

"We have to take a plane."

"What about school? Am I going to skip second grade?"

Jared doesn't answer. After he finishes packing his suitcase, he sits on it and zips it shut.

"Mommy can't live in New York right now," Jared explains slowly, twirling his fingers around and around. It's the weekend. He hasn't taken his white pill, so he talks more and he ruffles my hair and he tickles me all over until I fall on the floor screaming "Mercy, mercy me." It's Jared's favourite line from a song that Mommy played every morning when she was getting ready for work. We called it her morning music. Now, she only plays it at night. She can't go to work anymore.

Jared is humming that song. Then he's singing it. "Mercy, mercy me. Things ain't what they used to be."

"Jared, do you think if we go back to the Dominican Republic, Mommy will stop crying?" Every night before I go to sleep, I pray Mommy will wake up without any tears.

Jared shrugs. Then he reaches over and tickles me. "Come on Bubba, we gotta pack more stuff."

I giggle at the way Jared says 'stuff'. He giggles too. Then we start wrestling all over the clothes and books. Suddenly, Mommy's at the door.

"This place is chaos," she says. But she's not mad. She's sad. It's as if a heavy curtain has fallen all around her and Mommy can't find her way out. I want to pull that curtain down. Drag it off her and throw it away. But it's woven so tightly that there's no small hole that I can stick my finger in to start a rip.

Mommy gives Jared a look. It says, "You're in charge, mister."

Then she gives me a look. It says, "Don't let me down."

I want to give her a look that says, "Come play." But she turns and walks away.

"Chaos," says Mommy. "This world is chaos, right now."

I know what that word means because I have a small blue dictionary I keep with me at all times and I looked it up when Mommy first started saying it. Ms. Simon gave me the dictionary as a present at the end of first grade. I circle all the new words I learn. In the past three weeks there are a lot of them: obliterate, chaos, destruction and debris.

We are leaving in two days to go live on Mommy's island in the Caribbean. Mommy says she needs to be near her family and the sea and as far away from New York as she can get.

"We have to be safe," she whispers to me at night before she turns off the lights. "And there is nothing to keep me here."

There is no more office for Mommy to go to. No more

piles of paper to staple together and put in trial notebooks. The Courts are closed. The restaurant at the top of the Tower is gone. I wonder what had happened to Señor Hernandez. I ask Mommy this once and she looks at me as if her heart has been crushed again.

For the first couple weeks after September 11, Mommy drove us to school, and after she dropped Jared off early to his Special Math class for gifted kids, she took me to Burger King for breakfast.

I got a breakfast sandwich with egg and sausage and an orange juice. Mommy got tea and the newspaper. We sat in a booth across from each other as if we were going out to eat instead of waiting for school to start. She would glance at the headlines and wipe her eyes over and over. I talked about my favourite subject in school. Spelling. I had found something I was really good at. I loved words. I write them down on flash cards and carry them around and try to use them in sentences and it's fun.

One day I tell Mommy that I went to see Ms. Simon every day even though she isn't my teacher anymore.

"But why?" asks Mommy, looking up.

"Because she's right there. I can see her every day. And I love her."

"Oh," says Mommy. "You love her?"

I nod my head as I take a bite of my egg sandwich.

"How do you know you love her?"

I look at Mommy. That's a dumb question, but I can't say that out loud.

"Because I'm happy when I talk to her," I reply, which is true.

Mommy nods. I can feel her thinking about my answer. I want to ask, "Are you happy when you talk to me?" But I don't. Mommy is so sad all the time now that I don't want to know the answer. It might make me sad too.

14

elizabeth
MISSING PAPÍ

MONTHS AFTER PAPÍ HAS VANISHED in Neuva York, Mamí still cries every night. I slip out of my bed and sit by the little sea pool to stare at the stars just to get away from the sound of her tears. Her sadness is so huge it floods our room. Some nights, Mamí's tears spill out the window, down the hill and into Sosúa Bay. The water level in the Bay is rising drastically. Her tears are wet but they leave scorched embers behind, so hot I can't walk without feeling the burn of her grief under my feet.

Nothing I say or do can help her. Doña Maria tells me it takes time. That sadness and grief is a wounded animal that has to heal itself. But when I see Mamí sitting with her blank stare, I know it's up to me to fix this. Somehow. Maybe then I can cry for Papí, too. Right now I feel as if my tears are fake, as if missing Papí can't compare to Mamí's loss. So I keep quiet. But I miss him. I miss him all the time. I don't miss the money he sent every month that Mamí used to buy us clothes and shoes and for visits to the doctors and dentists and sometimes a movie in the new Playa Dorada cinema.

Mamí misses that. Or at least she worries about how we're going to pay for those things without Papí's Western Union money. Sometimes her sadness is interrupted with worry like she'd be washing clothes and suddenly exclaim, "How are we going to buy your school books next term, Elizabeth?" It's not as if she's talking to me. She doesn't even look at me. It's more like she's thinking of all the spaces Papí has left behind that we must fill by ourselves now.

What I miss the most is Papí's weekly phone calls. I would sit on the porch steps stretching the phone cord as far as it could go outside the house just to have Papí to myself for a few moments every Saturday afternoon. His voice sounded like he was right there on the porch with me teasing and laughing, drinking lemonade and eating Mamí's delicious kipes.

"How's my girl? Getting more bonita every day, eh?"

"No Papí, I'm still me. Gorda and fea."

"No, mi amor, you could never be fat and ugly. Tú eres muy bonita. But watch out for any tiguerito who might lead you the wrong way."

"As if!"

Papí would laugh and say, "Bueno, hija de mi vida." I would hand Mamí back the phone with a big smile. Mamí might be Papí's heart. But I was the joy of his life.

I never think about Papí on his last day facing the restaurant's burning walls and inhaling so much smoke that he can't even breathe. At least I don't think about it when I'm awake. But as soon as I fall asleep, I'm right there. The room gets hotter and hotter. The ceiling presses down on top of me, squeezing my chest flat until my I hear my bones crack like eggs dropped on the floor. It's so hot my skin peels off like bandages pulled fast and hard.

I feel Papí's pain as if it's my own. I strain my eyes to see
in the dark, to see some kind of light to lead me out of the
darkness. But there is nothing. Just the flames raging around me,
eating up all the air in the room.

Screams fill my ears. My own screams because I'm trapped. I
can't get out. But something outside is calling me and it only takes
one step, then two, then I'm gone.

When I wake up I'm tangled up in the sheets. My bed is
soaking wet with sweat or pee or tears. It doesn't matter which.
I drag my sheets off and slip downstairs to wash them in the big
outdoor sink before anyone else wakes up. My head feels hot
and my hair sticks to my neck. Red welts cover my skin. Deep
scratches run down my arms and legs and across my stomach.
I look like I've been in a fight. Or as if I've been clawing at my
body. Then I remember my dream and I sink down to the ground
and inhale the sweet scent of the earth to try and forget. Twice I
wake up clutching a charred piece of paper.

The first time I was so scared that I buried it. The second
time I stared at it for a long time. It was a menu. A menu from
the restaurant Papí worked at in Neuva York at the top of the
Twin Tower. How did I get it? The edges are so burnt they
crumble when I try to open the menu.

I put that one under my mattress. It's my last connection with
Papí that is only for me.

I like to think Papí went straight to heaven, no detour, no
stops, no falling, or choking to death. But I know it isn't true. I
know Papí's death was a hot and fiery one just like in the Bible

stories. I can feel what he felt. As if it's happening to me every night. And when I wake in the mornings, I cough up smoke. I try my best not to go to sleep at night. I stay up for a long time, laying in bed thinking of mermaids and the sea and my dream of being a lifeguard at Sosúa Beach so I can sit and watch the sea all day and save people who may be in danger. But no matter what I think about, when I finally close my eyes, I always end up in that suffocating box again with no way out.

So, I figure out that since I am being haunted by Papí it must be for a reason. And the reason, I think, is to help Mamí be happy again.

15

brandt

AND NOTHING CHANGES ...

OMMY SAYS WE ARE GOING to have a chance to start our lives over. I am not sure what that means. Do I get a different birthday? A new name? Our new life will start she says as soon as we board a plane for the Dominican Republic in JFK Airport in New York. We are shipping off tall, round containers that we're packing with our photo albums of baby pictures, and our favourite books and toys. Mommy packs sheets and towels in them and whenever Jared and I walk by the huge cardboard tubes that look like giant mouths, we toss in Pokémons, game cards, my stuffed animals, anything we do not want to leave behind.

Mommy says we have to leave some things because we can't take everything with us. I don't mind leaving the old TV and the shaky kitchen table, but I want to take my bunk bed and my desk with the little shelves above it and my furry green robe and dog slippers. Mommy says we are going to give all of those things away. Even my coat.

"We're not going to need a coat where we're going, mister," she says. "We're going to live on a hot island and everything will be different."

I look at Jared to see what he has to say about that. But he isn't looking at me or Mommy. He's busy reading a book as if we aren't even there.

I wish I could read like Jared so I could forget about moving and packing and giving away my bed. But I prefer movies, especially movies with a lot of music, and most especially *Grease*. Mommy says this is not a time to watch *Grease* even though I used to watch it every Saturday and Sunday and she didn't mind before.

I make sure that the *Grease* videotape is not on the donation pile though. I looked up the word "donation" so I know what it means, but all this giving away is confusing. Sometimes Mommy sits for ten minutes looking at a painting or a coffee mug as if whispering goodbye to it, before placing it in the donation pile.

The biggest goodbye is to Daddy. He agrees that us leaving New York is not a bad idea right now. He promises to come visit me and Jared every month and to call us every day. I also have to say a big goodbye to Ms. Simon and to all my friends at school. As we drive away from the school and I wave to my friends one last time, I sniff quietly so I won't start crying.

"Don't worry, Bubba," Mommy says. "You'll go to a new school in the Dominican Republic and you'll make new friends."

I want to tell Mommy that friends are not something you can just put on a donation pile and get new ones. Jared doesn't say anything but he doesn't have as many friends as me, so maybe he doesn't care.

After we get home, I sit watching Mommy zip up the last suitcases. I really wish I could watch *Grease* to feel better, but we don't have a TV anymore.

Then, Jared calls me over to our empty bedroom, and he's

smiling with his lips pressed together, which means that he is almost laughing. He's holding something behind his back.

"Guess what I got?"

"What?" I perk up.

"You have to guess."

"Your cow jacket?" I ask, because Jared loves his black and white fuzzy vest that looks, at least to me, just like a cow.

Jared frowns. "It's not a cow jacket." Then he smiles again, "But that's not it. Guess again."

"Tell me, tell me."

Jared shakes his head no.

"Okay, it's your Gameboy."

"Nope, not even close. And your guesses are lame. Try harder."

I crane my neck to see if I can get a peek around Jared's shoulder, but he twists away. "No cheating." He gives a little snort. "And everyone thinks you're such an angel. Ha!"

"Give me a clue."

"It's your favourite thing in the world."

"My favourite thing?"

Jared nods. "Guess."

"A dog?" I ask, because I have wanted a dog for so long and Mommy says we can't get one in New York City.

Jared gives a big sigh and shakes his head. "No, Bubba, I really don't think I'm holding a dog behind my back right now. No way, no how."

I laugh at the way Jared says 'no waaaay, no howwwwww'

stretching them out into a song. That's when I think of music, my favourite thing in the world.

"You got my *Grease* movie, Jared?" I ask, holding my breath.

"Close," Jared says, his smile growing wider.

I begin jumping up and down. Jared can't take my excitement any longer, so he whips out from behind his back his red and white portable CD player.

"Here," he says, handing me the black spongy headphones.

I look at him surprised. Jared never ever lets me touch his CD player.

"Put it on," he says. I carefully put on the headphones and sit down on the floor.

Jared sits next to me and he presses a button. And just like that, I am transported from our sad and empty apartment to a place filled up with colours and music. A huge smile bursts over my face.

'Summer Lovin' flows into '*Greased* Lightning' and on and on and I want to dance and sing but I stay on the floor just bobbing my head about as Jared sits next to me reading a book and checking on the CD player every once in a while. It's the perfect end to my last day in New York. I wonder if our new life is going to include music and movies and dancing and colours.

At the very end of all the *Grease* songs, Jared fast-forwards the CD to another song. When he presses Play I can't help but sing this song out loud even though I'm wearing headphones and I can't hear myself. Jared laughs and covers his ears with his hands as I sing.

He punches me on the arm and tells me to shush but he's kind of laughing still. This was one of Mommy's songs but I love it, too.

The next day, during the long plane ride, I keep singing that song over and over in my head. Everything is going to be okay, I think. Mommy will stop crying. I'll make new friends. Maybe Jared and Mommy won't get so mad at each other all the time. And maybe we'll have a real family again. Because that is all I really want.

But then the plane lands, and I walk through the big glass doors into a world that is hot, steamy and crowded with people. The sun is shining brightly and the sky is so blue and clear you can see everything in it – even tiny specks of planes flying high up going to other islands. But I don't notice that until a little later. Because first I see a tall, white-haired man walking toward us with a crinkly smile on his face and his arms wide open.

"Papa," Mommy cries, and rushes into his arms. And she's crying harder than ever. Almost choking on her hiccupy sobs.

I stand there next to Jared and I try to hold his hand so no one can see me. I don't want anyone to think I'm scared in this new place. Jared is shaking his head at Mommy. "What's wrong?" I ask.

"Nothing," he shrugs. "Nothing has changed."

I don't know what he means. But then our grandfather moves Mommy to his side and holds her with one arm. He opens his other arm toward us. I run right toward him, knowing without knowing that this is my brave, strong grandfather whom I have heard so many stories about, whom I spoke to on the telephone and who told me we can get a dog if I want when I move here.

"Welcome to your new home," he says.

I bury my entire body into my grandfather's arm. I look up and see Jared standing outside our circle. He has that "I don't care" look on his face: the look that everyone, especially Mommy, thinks is so rude. But I know what it really is, even if Mommy can't see.

"Jared, don't be rude to your grandfather," says Mommy, sounding embarrassed. "Come and hug him or at least say hello." She talks with that hint of fury in her voice.

And that's when I know, that although we have travelled for many miles by airplane, and have given away many of our things, and said goodbye to family and friends, that nothing has really changed. And I'm not sure if that's good or bad. Maybe a bit of both.

16

elizabeth
THE BOY ON THE CLIFF

NE NIGHT, AS MAMÍ WASHES the dinner dishes and I'm drying them, I notice that the moon is a magical ball of light sitting right on the ocean's surface like a visitor from outer space. I dash off without telling Mamí. I climb up the cliff, not even needing a flashlight because the moon's radiance is setting the red cliff on fire like hundreds of candles shimmering beneath my feet. I climb to the top and sit watching the moonbeams dancing on the water. The brilliant light slices through heaven and earth joining them together. Tonight, anything is possible. It's a night to dream. To make a moon wish. I close my eyes and turn my face toward the moon.

"I wish, I wish," I say loudly, speaking to the moon, "that Mamí will be happy again. Happy with me, happy to feel the sun, to look at the moon, to swim in the sea, to lace a red hibiscus in her hair and dance the merengue. I wish Mamí will be happy, even if Papí is not here."

I close my eyes tightly to seal my wish with the moonlight. When I open my eyes, a strange boy is standing right in front of me. I let out a small scream.

"Who are you?" I squeak out.

The boy doesn't answer. He looks like an ordinary boy with dark hair ruffling in the breeze and a dirty red hand that flings a pebble into the sea. But his eyes, when he looks at me, are as luminous as the moon.

I'm starting to wonder if he's some kind of magical boy who fell from the moon? Am I going loca like Mamí says? The boy is looking at me intently with eyes that seem to know things far beyond this cliff. Then he stares out at the ocean where there is nothing between the rest of the world and us.

"Who are you?" I ask him again. I ask him first in Spanish, and then French, and then English, hoping he'll know one of these languages.

Below the cliff, the water smacks itself against the rocks and sprays into the sky. The falling droplets scatter into little spots all over our clothes. The boy laughs. It's a musical and happy laugh. I laugh too as the waves continue to hit the rocks below and send more sparkling drops of water upon us.

I reach out and touch his arm to see if he's real. "Hola," I whisper. "My name is Elizabeth."

"Brandt," he whispers back. "My name is Brandt." His Spanish is shaky. I wonder if he's real or a dream or part of the history of this cliff.

As we sit looking at the moon and the ocean below, he turns to me and his eyes cloud over. He reaches a hand out to touch me and he says, so softly I almost don't hear him.

"Can I join in your wish?"

"What?" I ask him. "What do you want?" It sounds as if he wants to be part of my wish.

He speaks a little louder and his voice sings on the waves and I hear him just fine. "Can I join in your wish? I wish, that my mother will be happy again, too."

I lean forward on the boulder to look more closely at him.

"Is your mother sad?" I ask.

He nods.

"Why is she sad?"

"The Towers fell down," he says.

I nod my head, but I'm not sure that I understand. Is he talking about what happened at the World Trade Center? Or is he from another planet, like the boy in The Little Prince, which we are reading in French class at school?

"The fires," Brandt says, "they're still burning. And the smoke drifts over our houses filling our noses and eyes with debris."

I ask him what "debris" means. He says it's a new word he has learned since the fall of the towers. He pulls out a little blue book from his pocket and he turns the pages until he finds what he is looking for. Then he reads to me in English under the light of the moon that "debris" means "wreckage" or "rubble."

"Oh," I say. "Wreckage doesn't sound good." Even if I don't know exactly what it means.

He nods his head. "I wish my mother would be happy again," he whispers to me, and there is a splintering in his voice as if pages of his book are being turned but no answers can be found.

I take Brandt's hand and squeeze it. He is a lot younger than me but his eyes are not. The look in Brandt's eyes is deeper than the sea when I dive down and look for mermaid treasure. "Where are you from?" I ask him.

He says he comes from the north where snowflakes fall in

winter and his breath turns icy and wind snaps at his heels and there is no thought of swimming at all because the waters are frozen. I cannot imagine such a thing.

Brandt tells me his book is to help him learn as many words as possible so he can understand what everyone is saying. He sounds very sure of himself.

I nod my head again, but I don't agree with this. A word can mean so many different things to different people. Like the words "dream" or "love." Or one thing can have different names. Like this very cliff we are standing on.

Hundreds of years ago, the Taino Indians called this cliff Iguana Hill because of all the large lizards that lived on the dry bushes. The Spanish conquistadores who came along and destroyed many of the Tainos had their own name for this hill. They called it La Puntilla, or the small point. The Jewish refugees who came from Europe during World War II and settled in Sosúa called this cliff, Mizpah, or watchtower because from here they could look out and see the ocean separating them from their old country.

Now, the Dominicanos, who are like me, a mixture of the Tainos, the Spanish colonials, and the enslaved Africans who worked the plantations here, we call the cliff, El Mirador, which means "the lookout." All of these different names and histories for one red cliff. It shows you mightn't understand someone if you don't know his whole story, which is how I'm feeling about this Brandt kid.

But I don't tell Brandt this. Maybe where he's from words

mean one thing only. And anyway, I can't bear to tell him, because I want his smile to return. I want him to laugh again. "Tell me more about yourself," I say to him.

He sits down on the rock next to mine and tosses one more pebble into the sea.

17

brandt
MEETING ELIZABETH

HAVE A BROTHER," I tell the Elizabeth girl. We are on the hill near Grand Pop's home. It's a rocky hill with small bushes of prickly leaves and purple flowers and you can see everything from the top.

"A brother?" she asks, sounding amazed. "I always wanted a brother. Or a sister."

"Why?" I ask.

"To talk to. To tell him about the moon and the mermaids."

"With brothers, it's sometimes like that. But not usually."

"Does your brother talk to you about these kinds of things?"

"My brother's very smart. He tells me about all kinds of things. But I can't speak with him a lot."

"Why not?" she demands.

"He says I annoy him. It's my voice. And all my questions. My humming, too, and if I tap my feet he gets very angry and yells at me and says that I'm doing it on purpose to drive him nuts."

Her hands are on her hips. "I don't think I like your brother, Brandt."

I look right into her eyes which are wide and slanted and brown like the rocks. "You have to like him," I say. "Or else I can't like you."

"You like him?" she asks, shocked. "Even though he yells at you just for tapping your feet?"

I smile at this fierce girl. "My brother held my hand when The Towers fell down. He walked me home and didn't tell me to be quiet. And when we had to come to this island to live with our grandfather, my brother tickled me and told me everything would be okay."

"Your grandfather?" she asks.

"Yes, he lives over there." I point to our home.

"That's Señor Oscar Hess' home," she says it like she's talking about someone famous.

"You know my grandfather?"

"He's a legend here. I don't really know his story. But Doña Maria told me it's the bravest, saddest story she's ever heard. And he's a true hero."

"My Grand Pop?"

Elizabeth nods. "Yes. He escaped something terrible. At least that's what I heard."

I think this Elizabeth girl is making up stories but I don't mind. There's something about Grand Pop that is a big secret. When I asked him what he did as a boy far away in Germany, he said his life started when he arrived here on the island and he can only tell me about this life with my grandmother.

"My grandmother died a long time ago," I tell Elizabeth.

She gives me that look Jared does like, "Duh!"

"I see Señor Hess sometimes," says Elizabeth. "He rides his bicycle and takes walks with his binoculars to look at the birds. Sometimes I see him sitting up here staring at the sky and I leave because he's praying or something."

"I don't know about the birds or the binoculars but Grand Pop does have a big blue bicycle."

"So, you'll be my neighbour." Her smile is pretty and white like the moon. Then she frowns and adds, "I don't know about your brother, though."

"My brother can't say what he really means and the wrong things always come out of his mouth," I explain.

"How do you know that?" she asks.

"Because I just know. And when I was little and no one could hear me speak, my brother was the only one who could hear me."

I imagine that this cold, icy place where Brandt comes from people like him can read minds. They can feel each other's thoughts and they don't have to speak at all. I think over this for a moment. That is not so different from here. I can feel what Mamí and Doña Maria are thinking even when they don't say a word.

"Okay, I'll like your brother, Brandt. Since you like him. I'd want a brother who holds my hand when something bad happens."

"Yup. That's exactly the brother he is. Once, it was my birthday and Mommy was driving us to a restaurant for a special dinner. She got upset with me and shouted and I was almost crying. Jared was playing his Gameboy in the front seat. Without even looking up he said, 'Don't make Brandt cry on his birthday,' in a real strong voice. Mommy stopped right away whatever she had been saying. It was a perfect birthday after that."

"It sounds like your mother and brother are the same," says

Elizabeth.

"My mother says I'm her joy," I tell her.

"I thought your mother was sad."

"She is right now. It's up to me to make her happy again."

"I know what you mean. It's up to me to help my Mamí be happy, too."

"What happened to your mother?" I ask.

Elizabeth's voice gets very small. "I think she blames me for my Papí dying. She said I put a curse on my Papí."

"A curse?"

Elizabeth shakes her head. "I didn't."

I look at this Elizabeth girl with the long black hair and the sad kind of smile and I wish I knew what she was talking about. But one thing I learned from being with Jared is that it's better not to ask too many questions. You don't have to understand every single little thing to get what's right or wrong with someone.

So, we both look out over the ocean. The wind is picking up and I can hear the rustling leaves of the trees nearby, which Grand Pop told me were banana trees. I can't wait to see real bananas growing on a tree.

A large cloud slides over the moon blocking out all the light. The sky changes from dark blue to pure black. Elizabeth and I watch silently until the sea vanishes into the dark sky completely and everything is one. And there in that silent night I feel how alone she really is.

18

elizabeth
TÍO'S GIFT

ODAY, I RECEIVED A GIFT from Tío Franco, who lives in Moca and only comes down to Sosúa to sell his artwork to the tourist shops. My gift is a mermaid sculpture made out of green metal. "Beautiful art makes life's sorrows bearable," he says as he hammers a green metal hook into the wooden beam across the doorway. "It's to remind you of your life before legs."

"Thank you, Tío," I tell him. "It is beautiful. Like a butterfly mermaid."

Mamí shakes her head at him.

Tío Franco plucks the mermaid out of my hands and hangs it. "Ta da!" The thin, metal sculpture spins in circles. The mermaid's arms are open wide as if she's trying to catch a wave outside the window.

"I love it, Tío." I hug him and feel the first bit of happiness seeping back into me.

"Come," says Tío Franco, looking at Mamí. "I will take you both to Sosúa Beach.

My heart leaps up and I want to say yes, please, take me to the beach, but I see the dark look on Mamí's face. "How can you ask us that? It wouldn't be appropriate. We're still grieving."

"You can't stay locked up forever," he says.

Mamí looks up at Tío and shakes her head. "I can. I have

plenty of work to do here." She looks at me and I squirm on my chair. "But take Elizabeth."

I run to hug her but her arms don't reach around me. "Come with us, Mamí," I beg. But I already know that Mamí will not swim in the sea, or laugh at the swinging mermaid on the wall, or even just sit on the sand and look at the water. Mamí flicks her hand at us like we are two mosquitoes bothering her. "Go on, both of you," she says in a sad, tired voice.

I stand still for a moment wondering if there's anything I can say to Mamí to pull her out of her lonely tunnel. Before I can think of anything, Tío yanks my hair and I look up at him. His eyes are not as twinkly as before, but he pushes me gently toward the door. "Go get your swim suit, little mermaid, the sea waits for no one."

I run inside to change into my swim suit with the red flowers. I grab a beach towel and walk hand-in-hand with Tío Franco to Sosúa Beach. The sidewalk vendors are all out selling their brightly-coloured paintings, smelly cigars, gleaming bottles of rum and pretty straw bags.

Some of them wave hello to Tío and ask him when he is bringing his artwork for them to sell. Tío stops at different shops and examines the wooden sculptures until finally he picks up one of a fish, which he holds up and turns it all around and then exclaims in a soft breath, "It's perfect, Elizabeth."

I look at the crowded shop filled from sandy floor to tarp covered galvanized roof with paintings, sculptures, hanging mobiles and hundreds of knick-knacks. How did Tío Franco pluck one perfect thing out of the bunch? When I ask him all he says is, "You just know."

Tío happily pays a few pesos for it and the shopkeeper wraps it up snugly in old newspaper.

"It's for your Mamí," says Tío.

"Mamí isn't going to like that fish," I tell Tío before I run off down the hill. When he catches up with me, I add. "Because it doesn't change anything."

"You're right, Elizabeth. It doesn't change anything that happened. It's just to give hope."

"But she doesn't have hope anymore, Tío." I know it's true as soon as I say the words and it makes me stop running and slow all the way down.

"Everyone has hope, mi amor. Otherwise they can't live. Your Mamí hoped she'd be a famous salsa dancer when she was your age. She also hoped for a little girl after she married your Papí."

"She didn't become a famous salsa dancer."

"No, but she got you," says Tío and pulls my hair.

Tío and I walk past the vendors selling beach jewellery made from sea glass and ribbons. The sea glass looks like it's winking at us.

"I used to hope that one day I'd live right near the sea," I say. "And now I do. Even though I didn't know how that was going to happen."

Tío opens his palms up like, "See?"

I giggle. "Remember when Mamí told me we'd go live with Doña Maria, I was so mad. I didn't want to leave Moca. But then we got here and, poof, my dream had come true. I was living in a house right next to the sea."

"I remember how you cried and cried, 'Oh, I don't want to go. Don't make me.'"

I press my lips together so I wouldn't remind Tío how he had hugged me and cried when I was leaving, too. It seemed like so long ago. All that crying for nothing.

As if he knows exactly what I'm thinking, Tío lifts my hand up in the air and twirls me around dancing a salsa on the sand. But even with all the sunshine breaking through the leaves of the trees, and even with the blue sea near our feet, Tío's smile is really only half a smile and my dance is missing steps. It's hard to be happy when someone you love is sad.

When we finish dancing, we spread our towels on the white sand and tuck our feet under us. The ocean races right up to our towels and we scoot back so we don't get wet.

Tío lays back on his towel and puts his hat over his face. "Hasta luego," he says. "My brain needs a rest."

"Tío?" I shake his arm.

After a while I hear a loud snore. I tiptoe off the towel and run across the hot sand into the cool clear sea. I point my hands above my head and slide into the blue waves. I lunge straight down to touch the soft, sandy bottom, flicking the waves with my mermaid tail. I'm alive down here where the silver fish swim by and I can hear the gurgling of the ocean in my ears. I've always been a mermaid. You know who and what you are, no matter what anyone else says.

I swim up through another wave and I'm far far out. Tío Franco is just a speck on the sand under his green hat. Poor Tío Franco. He loves to paint all day long. But everyone in the family says he's wasting his time.

"Get a real job," Mamí tells him.

My grandfather, Abuelo Alejandro, is disappointed that Tío is not an engineer. He says Tío is lazy. He complains that Tío Franco is always looking at the stars.

But Tío has a workshop full of surprises he creates every day. Wooden masks with colourful feathers. Mobiles that spin and chime in the breeze. Paintings of women with flowers in their hair. I can't go in the studio barefooted because the floor is covered with paint and loose feathers, stray buttons and glass beads.

When I tell Abuelo about what I see in Tío's studio, Abuelo just snaps that it doesn't put food on the table.

I pop out of the water and feel raindrops on my shoulders. The sky is dark with heavy clouds. I hook my fingers together and lean into a wave, body surfing all the way to the shore where I land with a swoosh right near Tío's feet. He leaps up and shouts, "It's a mermaid, a real life mermaid!"

"You fell asleep, Tío," I jump up and say with my hands on my hips.

Tío runs into the water and ducks under a wave. He pops up sputtering in the rain. "How do you mermaids deal with all this water?"

I laugh at my crazy Tío. "It's our life."

Later, as we walk up the hill toward the house, I think about Mamí and her never-ending sighs. I remember something my fifth grade maths teacher called the 'missing factor'. She said that an equation can be solved with the 'missing factor'.

Maybe that's what Papí is. He's the missing factor in our lives. Without him, Mamí has no husband. I have no father. Tío has no brother-in-law to play dominoes with. And Doña Maria, she already has her own missing factor and doesn't need another one. The missing factor is everything. Maybe what we need is a new equation. Not to forget about Papí, but to have new hope.

"What are you thinking about, Elizabeth?" asks Tío as we walk carefully balancing our turban towels on our heads like genies who just popped out of a lamp.

"Everything, Tío."

He raises his eyebrows into his turban. "Let me know when you figure everything out, okay?" He says it quite seriously.

I smile at my uncle. "I will."

19

brandt
THE LAUGHING CLIFF

WO DAYS LATER I RETURN to the top of the cliff again and this time I'm with my grandfather. Elizabeth is sitting on the edge of a rock peering over the side as if looking for something. I introduce her to Grand Pop and she calls him Señor Oscar Hess, and looks down as she shakes his giant wrinkled hand.

"You are Doña Maria's niece," he says, with a bow.

"Si, Señor." On the outside she's all proper and polite but I can tell that inside she's jumping up and down. It's the way she hugs her arms close to her body as if she's afraid she'll throw them around Grand Pop or hug the sky or something.

Grand Pop touches me on my head. "You're making friends, eh?" he rumbles in a deep voice.

I look up at my grandfather. He has the same colour eyes as me. Jared and Mommy have brown eyes and I have what Mommy calls hazel eyes, which she says is the colour of the sky before a storm, or as Jared says, the colour of laundry water before the rinse cycle.

"We made a wish together," I tell Grand Pop. "A very important wish."

Elizabeth nods her head hard in agreement. "We're going to share a dream."

Grand Pop looks from me to Elizabeth and back again.

"Wishes and dreams come true more often when they are shared," he says, in a serious voice.

That makes me and Elizabeth smile.

"Cool," says Elizabeth.

"Double cool with oreos and milk," I add.

Elizabeth's forehead twists in a funny scowl. "This is serious, Brandt."

Grand Pop laughs out this roaring sound like a subway car racing into a tunnel. We look at him amazed. He's laughing like he hasn't laughed in a long time and both me and Elizabeth start laughing, too.

"Everything will be okay," says Grand Pop when he's stopped the loud freight train noises. "As long as you can always laugh at the end."

"Like in cartoons," I say.

"Exactly," says Grand Pop.

Elizabeth doesn't look so sure. We're all quiet for a while watching the sky and listening to the booming sound of the waves on the rocks.

"Like mermaids," Elizabeth finally says. "We can laugh at the mermaids that spin in the wind and dance on the waves."

Me and Grand Pop look at each other and he raises his eyebrows at me and wiggles them just like Jared does. I want to burst out laughing again but I don't.

"Yes," I tell Elizabeth solemnly. "Just like that."

Grand Pop tilts his head and looks at us without saying a word.

20

elizabeth
MAGICAL MOONBEAMS

WISH THERE WAS A MAGIC SEED I could plant that would sprout a tree of happiness so my Mamí and Brandt's mother could eat the fruit and just be happy.

I meet Brandt's mother one day at the beach and she looks just like my Mamí. Her eyes are focused on something far away and although she smiles when Brandt and I bring her sea shells I can tell she is smiling just to be polite and not because she sees how pretty, pink and swirly they are.

That's when I had the idea, like Tío had suggested, that beautiful art makes sadness better. So, Brandt is making a shell necklace for his mother. I'm making one of moonbeams for mine.

"How can you string moonbeams?" Brandt asks, when I tell him.

"It's a secret," I whisper. But I am dancing all over the sand and I cannot wait to tell Brandt. He is my friend now, and we go everywhere together. He doesn't speak a lot, but when he does, it is usually something very important and true. I forget he is four years younger than me.

Brandt doesn't ask me to tell him the secret, probably because he knows I'm bursting to tell him and I will anyway. He waits patiently and I wonder how can he be so still and sure I will tell. Why isn't he urging me to spill the secret? But before I can think about that anymore, I sit down in a splash of sand next to him. "Okay, I'll tell you," I lean closer to him.

Brandt smiles at me and I feel cheated somehow as if I'm doing exactly as he planned except I don't think Brandt is some kind of trickster.

"Mermaids make their necklaces from moonbeams," I tell him. "The moon's light glimmers on rocks for hundreds of years and casts them into shiny pebbles. Only mermaids know which ones of the pebbles are moonbeams." With that I empty my shorts pocket onto the sand. A cascade of black sparkling pebbles falls at his feet.

"These are moonbeams?" he asks, picking one up gingerly.

I nod. "There are plenty there and if you want to use some for your mother's necklace, you can. Shells are pretty and your mother would like it, but I think the moonbeams have a special magic."

Brandt rubs his fingers over the small black stones. "How do you make a necklace out of these moonbeams?" he asks. "You can't put a string through them like you can with shells that have tiny holes."

"I know," I shake my head, "but we can think of something."

"Ok," Brandt says. We both sit looking at the sparkling moonbeams for a little while not speaking. The waves are gentle today and the coconut trees sway just a little in the slight breeze. The air is filled with the smell of flowers from the jasmine trees nearby.

"Why does it have to be a necklace?" asks Brandt, suddenly breaking the silence. "Why don't we make something else with the moonbeams?"

I didn't think of that. "Something else?"

"Yes, something else. Made from moonbeams."

"Oh."

We stare at the black moonbeams that seem to flash with inner light.

"But what?" I ask. For once I'm stumped.

We continue sitting and staring at them. Then we hear the sand swishing as feet come sliding up - it's Jared and he has a Gameboy in his hand.

The first time I met Jared, Brandt's older brother, my heart almost stopped. It was like I was seeing the present and the future all at the same time. Well, okay, he was really cute, but there was something else about him. Something fragile, which he hid from everyone with harsh words and curt replies.

We tell Jared our dilemma about the moonbeams. At first, Jared screws up his eyebrows and gives a snort. I can tell he doesn't believe in the moonbeams. His foot touches one and Brandt gathers them closer to us and looks up at his brother. Jared doesn't believe in any kind of magic. He's one of those people, like my Mamí, who can't believe in something unless they are actually touching it.

"It's a present for Mommy," says Brandt. "So she'll be happy again."

The look on Jared's face is all icy and cold - as if he's not sure how to feel about that. He stands there for a moment, then plops down on the sand and turns back to his game. "Good luck," he mumbles. "It's a dumb idea though, you know that, right? You can't make anyone happy, not even with moonbeams - they have to be happy by themselves."

Brandt and I look at each other - I can tell he's as stunned as I am. That can't be true. Of course, we can help someone to be happy – after all, I'm happy being with Brandt and swimming in the sea and looking at Tío Franco's paintings and mermaid sculptures. I can help Mamí be happy too.

"Well, we can try anyway," says Brandt, speaking out loud in answer to my thoughts.

I nod my head.

Jared keeps clicking away at his Gameboy. After a few minutes he looks at us. "Well, if you want to make the moonbeams into a present, why don't you fill up a glass jar with them and put flowers in the top of the jar, so they can be a vase of moonbeam flowers. That way you don't have to glue anything or try to string them together."

Brandt and I look at each other, then at Jared, who is still clicking away on his video game as if he hasn't just solved our problem with a genius idea. But as I watch Jared, I see the beginning of a smile tugging at the corners of his lips. At first it is a little smirk, but then I clearly see dimples in his cheeks as he tries not to smile and fails.

I burst out laughing and Jared hangs his head to try and hide his face. I poke him in his arm and he looks up with a full blast grin and it's the most beautiful face I've ever seen. His smile has completely transformed his usual scornful look. I feel a light flowing right through me straight to Jared or maybe it's from Jared straight to me, but then and there I feel something for the first time ever. I don't know. It feels like a bird is trying to fly around in my heart.

Jared goes back to his Gameboy and I stand up with Brandt shaky at this new feeling I have. I look over my shoulder at Jared as Brandt and I set out to find two pretty glass jars to fill up with our moonbeams and he's still smiling.

21

brandt
HOPE IN A VASE

"Y OUR BROTHER IS PRETTY COOL," says
Elizabeth as we make our way through the beach
vendors asking for empty glass jars. "How'd he
come up with such a great idea, just like that?" She
snaps her fingers.

I don't answer her because I'm thinking that if Jared is so smart
and knows everything then . . . .

"Do you think it's true what he said?" I ask Elizabeth. "That
this present won't make our mothers happy?" I've stopped
walking and I'm staring at the sand. For the first time ever I feel
lost. Even though Elizabeth is right in front of me and Jared is
nearby and I know exactly where I am. Maybe lost is a place that
you disappear to when you feel sad.

Elizabeth puts a hand on my shoulder. It's warm and sandy
and a little sticky too. With her other hand she pulls out a
handful of the black moonbeams from her pocket. "Look at
these, Brandt. They're amazing. Our mothers will love them."

I stare at the polished stones that are reflecting the light
streaming through the trees above us.

"Maybe my Mamí won't start singing all around the house
like she used to do when Papí was here, but she'll smile and start
doing things with me again. At least I hope so."

I reach out a finger and touch one of the moonbeams.

"Maybe my mother will count the stars with me again."

Elizabeth slides the moonbeams into her pocket. "I bet she will. Even Jared thinks it might work. Otherwise he wouldn't be helping us."

I agree. Jared doesn't ever make vases or necklaces for anyone. "I'm going to tell Mommy that Jared helped too. That'll definitely make her happy."

With this new hope, Elizabeth and I scour every beach vendor selling art and straw bags, cigars and cold drinks. We ask them all for anything that could hold magical moonbeam flowers. "It's got to be the right kind of vase," says Elizabeth turning down dirty jars or ones with chipped rims. Finally, we find two glass jars that look like vases with thin flowing edges and curvy sides. We carry them back to where Jared is still sitting under a coconut tree playing his game.

As Jared looks on from the corner of his eye, Elizabeth and I get to work. I hum as I pour sand and sprinkle shells and place the black stones in the jar. The pattern of black and pink looks cool and mysterious like the colours in my *Grease* movie. In my head I'm saying over and over. "Mommy will like this. Mommy will like this." It becomes a chant and I don't realize I'm saying it out loud until Elizabeth and Jared laugh and I look at them surprised, then we all laugh.

Jared makes his usual snippy comments as he glances back and forth between his game and our vases, but even Elizabeth seems to realize that he doesn't mean them. It's like listening to a hungry bird chirping away for its mother to feed it, and as long as you know it's just a hungry bird, the chirping doesn't annoy you.

Finally, I give my jar a shake to settle some shells into place. I raise it up and twirl it around so that the light sparkles off the glass and catches the moonbeams. Elizabeth is biting her lip as she leans over her jar and trickles sand through her fingers into her jar.

As we get closer to finishing, Jared stops playing his game and watches us. He tries to act as if what we're doing is not important, but then he asks if he can put the last moonbeam in each vase.

Elizabeth doesn't say a word as she tips her jar toward him so he can drop in the last moonbeam. It's Jared who's tall enough to reach up and pluck a pretty red hibiscus flower for Elizabeth's vase and a majestic orange flower for mine. When the vases of moonbeam flowers are ready, we start the walk up the hill from the beach and along the curving path back to our homes.

I walk slowly, holding my jar carefully, not spilling any sand or shells or tipping over the flower on top. I start talking to myself in my head again. "Please let this work."

"Hey Bubba, watch where you're going."

I almost walk right into Jared because I've been thinking so hard.

"What are you mumbling?" asks Jared "Abra ca dabra?"

Elizabeth and I giggle.

"Remember the fire in the church?" I ask Jared.

Jared frowns.

"What fire?" asks Elizabeth.

"There was a fire and Mommy went dashing up to the front of the church and pushed open the sanctuary door to rescue Jared."

Jared snorts. "Wasn't me who needed to be saved, though." He has a fierce look on his face when he stares at me.

Elizabeth's eyes are bouncing between me and Jared. "What happened?"

"Well, I'm having that same feeling. The one where the smoke fills up my ears and mouth and I can't breathe. I'm feeling that again right now."

Elizabeth's eyes are opened wide. "I used to feel like that too."

We all look at each other and for one long moment we're trapped together in a dark, smoky choking place. It's Jared who takes charge. He presses his lips together. "She's gonna like it, Bubba. And so will your mother, Elizabeth," he adds softly.

Elizabeth eyes light up and I think it's because of the way Jared said her name. I don't think he's ever said her name before and it sounds musical and pretty and I never knew a word could sound like that coming from Jared.

As if he wants to see her light up again, he says, "Our mothers will definitely love your presents, don't worry."

We start back up the road with Elizabeth bouncing along laughing happily, me smiling at my vase, and Jared, for the first time ever since we arrived here, walking in front, eyes ahead, head held high.

22

elizabeth
A PEBBLE IN A HURRICANE

INCE MEETING BRANDT, I've become a regular visitor to Señor Oscar's house on the cliff. I love the huge picture windows that slide open to let in the entire sky. There is a shady courtyard in the middle of the house with a large flowering frangipani tree spreading its beauty over the gray rocks that are large enough for sitting on. The courtyard is where Señor Oscar sits and reads in the early morning as the sun rises.

"It's my den of contemplation," he told us.

Brandt immediately took out his little blue dictionary and looked up "contemplation." It means "thought and reflection," he says. Now, I always think of the courtyard as a private room for deep thought.

When we arrive at their home, Brandt's and Jared's mother is sitting on the gallery under a large umbrella with a magazine in her lap. She looks like she's sleeping except her eyes are wide open. Tall green plants in brown earth pots line the perimeter of the gallery. The dark blue sea rises to the left and the rugged green mountains jut skyward on the right. Despite all the glow, I can feel the emptiness around her as if there's no sea or mountains or plants or us.

Brandt coughs and she looks up with a quizzical expression. Jared, Brandt and I all walk toward her, although Jared has slowed down and is now hovering in the back like he's putting on brakes.

Brandt stretches out his arms and hands over the vase, saying something I can barely hear.

"He made it for you," Jared speaks up.

Their mother takes the vase and holds it like a torch above her head looking at the bottom of the glass jar. "What is it?"

Brandt is solemn and hopeful at the same time. "It's a vase of moonbeam flowers. A present for you from me and Jared. And Elizabeth." He looks over at me and I wink but my wink is like a pebble in a hurricane. It gets blown out of the water.

Their mother is not smiling. "Oh," is all she says. She flicks her hand at the table behind her. "Just put it over there honey. I'll look at it later." And she turns back to the magazine she's not reading and the view she's not seeing.

"Ok," Brandt says, bravely, but the sound of his voice in that one single word breaks my heart. I can't even look at him. I inch backward, scared at the silence. I swear I will cry right then and there. I can feel the sadness seeping into Brandt, a deathly kind of sadness that will drown him. His mother isn't even looking around to witness her son's heart breaking in two.

Then, I feel someone pushing me aside. It's Jared. He grabs the vase with both hands. I gasp as he raises it above his head, shouting, "Just forget it! It's not for you." Then, Jared hauls the beautiful vase of flowers and moonbeams against the wall, like a cricket bowler. Like a fisherman throwing a line far out. Like an angry, mean, torn apart animal trying to destroy itself.

The vase shatters into a million pieces. And that's when I cry.

23

brandt

AND THEN SILENCE COVERED ALL ...

ARED ISN'T SPEAKING to anyone, not even me. It was like the broken vase stole his words and took everything from him. There was silence all around Jared and the silence seeped past him to me and then to Elizabeth because it had been the same thing with her own mother.

I went with Elizabeth to Doña Maria's home and Elizabeth's mother started asking her right away, "What are these rocks and shells doing here?" She pointed to the vase of moonbeam flowers.

"Rocks and shells?" Elizabeth murmured. I had never heard my friend speak so sadly. "It's moonbeams. It's a gift."

Elizabeth's mother's voice softened, "Thank you, mi amor, but I hope it doesn't make a mess for me to have to clean up. You didn't put any sand in there, did you?"

Elizabeth shook her head, although she had put quite a lot of sand in there. She just stared at her mother.

"Why are you looking at me so strangely, hija. Do you want some dinner?"

Elizabeth shook her head again. I reached over and squeezed her hand. We walked side by side out to the little cove at the back door. There was a tree with tiny yellow flowers swaying in the breeze.

"Well that didn't go like we hoped," said Elizabeth.

"Yeah. Not at all."

Then my happy, mermaid, hopeful new best friend burst into a thousand tears that fell like little drops of stones on my hands. I didn't know what to say. I pulled my knees close to my chest and just sat by her side.

The days passed and Mommy did the same thing every day. She made us breakfast, did laundry, read the newspaper or watched CNN and then sat on the gallery reading a book or magazine. Some days she went to town to buy groceries with Grand Pop. It was like Mommy was not living but just floating from one activity to another one, without seeing or hearing or feeling anything.

She complained about Jared more now because he was not speaking to her at all. She made a lot of phone calls to find a psychiatrist in Puerto Plata who could 'help' Jared.

"That child needs to see someone," she kept repeating.

Grand Pop said, "He does not need to see anyone outside this house."

I knew that Grand Pop meant that Jared needed to see Mommy and Mommy needed to see Jared. And by 'see' he meant with more than their eyes. But Mommy didn't get it. She insisted that she needed to find a good counsellor who could talk to Jared.

Grand Pop looked at me and I looked back at him. How come what was so clear to us was so far from Mommy's vision?

One evening when I couldn't take the stand off in our house

anymore, I walk up to the cliff. The sun is going down in the ocean in a splash of colours. Even in the dark I can hear the sound of the sea. In New York, I didn't have this constant, never-ending sound of music that feels like a huge thing. Huger than buildings that reach the sky. Huger than planes crashing into lives. Huger than every single thing I can imagine. There is no confusion or misunderstandings or sadness by the sea and it is the only place I want to be right now.

Soon, I hear footsteps climbing the hill and I know without looking around that it's Elizabeth. She isn't springing along as usual. She's plodding and trudging, sending dust flying where before she glided over the clay rocks.

She doesn't speak to me. Her silence is different than the silence of Jared's anger or Mommy's sadness. Her silence is like frozen icicles.

"We're in a precarious situation," I say, as the sky darkens and the colours disappear.

"Precarious?" she asks.

"Yes, I learned that word today - I heard Mommy telling a doctor that Jared is in a precarious situation."

"Well?" asks Elizabeth.

"It means dangerous," I tell her.

Elizabeth's voice rings out sharply, "Is he?"

"Yes," I say. "We all are in a dangerous situation right now."

Elizabeth heaves a big sigh.

"What're we going to do?" But she isn't speaking to me. She's looking up at the stars that are popping out of the dark, blue sky like dazzling coins.

"Maybe we can go on a journey," Elizabeth muses out
loud as she continues looking at the stars. "And we can bring
back something truly magical, like from the bottom of the sea,
something so special that our mothers can't help but notice it and
be excited and happy about it."

I bite my lip. "A journey?" I don't understand how that can
help our mothers.

"Yes, a journey, I heard about some dwarves who live in the
hills of Jarabacoa and we can travel there and speak to them. I bet
they know magic."

I stay quiet. I'm not sure about Elizabeth's idea.

Well, if not a journey," she says, "then what're we going to
do?"

"What're we going to do about what?" asks a deep voice.

Elizabeth shrieks and practically jumps off the boulder she's
sitting on.

Grand Pop chuckles. "It's only me." He lumbers up and sits
down on his favourite rock.

Mommy said Grand Pop has been through the worst of times.
And yet he's still smiling. In fact, he's always smiling. I wonder
what the worst of times mean, but Mommy said she would tell
me when I'm older.

"Well, children, what is it you want to do?"

Elizabeth speaks up. "Our wish is not coming true."

"Ah," he says, with a smile in his voice, "I remember when
you both decided to share a wish. What was it, if you don't mind

me asking?"

"It's a wish for Mommy," I say.

"And for my Mamí too," says Elizabeth.

Grand Pop's staring up at the sky turning his head this way and that as if trying to count the silvery coins.

"We wish our mothers would be happy again," says Elizabeth, and I hear deep down tears in her voice.

"Ahhh," says Grandfather. "That's a great wish."

"Yes, but we tried to make it come true and it didn't work," I explain.

Grandfather nods. "The moonbeam flowers, right?"

"Yes, but they didn't even notice. I thought Mamí would laugh or something."

"Now, Jared is sadder than before, because it was his idea to give them the moonbeam flowers in the first place," I add.

The idea that our plan had not only failed, but added to the sadness around us, makes us quiet.

"So, what's next?" Grandfather asks, breaking the silence in a matter-of-fact voice.

"A journey," says Elizabeth. "Like in books, only ours will be real and we will travel to the mountains of Jarabacoa, where there are waterfalls and a big river and we will find the dwarves who live there and maybe they have magic we can learn from them."

Grand Pop doesn't say anything.

"Or maybe a journey to the bottom of the sea for mermaid treasure," Elizabeth keeps talking. "Something so amazing they can't help but notice it."

In Grand Pop's silence, I hear him thinking. He's contemplating something deeply. I feel it in the air.

Elizabeth starts to speak again, but I put my hand on her arm. "Shhhh," I whisper. I keep my hand on her arm. She turns to me and then looks at Grand Pop. Even in the darkness with just the glimmering stars flickering above us, we can see he is miles away, years and years from here.

"He's praying," whispers Elizabeth. "I've seen him before sitting just like that and looking just this way."

A big wave smacks against the rocks below and sends a drizzling rain of sea drops all over us. The sea refuses to be left out of anything.

Elizabeth and I giggle. It's our first laugh in a long time.

Grandfather clears his throat. Then he takes a deep breath. He looks at Elizabeth then at me for a long while not saying anything. I sit not moving, knowing that somehow Grand Pop is measuring us. I don't know what for, but under his steady gaze my heart beats fast.

"I'll tell you a story," he finally says. "A true story."

The dark, purple sky shelters us as Elizabeth and I settle down to listen.

24

brandt

GRANDFATHER'S STORY

here were three brothers, Marius, Oscar, and David, the youngest. We lived in Germany, in a small village near the border of the Black Forest. Marius played the piano for hours every day. David built kites that flew for hours. Oscar, that's me, painted pictures of the sky with clouds that looked like his brothers and his mother and father.

Marius married a girl and moved into her parents' home so they could save for their own home. I was seventeen and was the wild lad of the village, painting people's portraits for a fee. David read huge physics books and studied to be an engineer. David fixed things. That was his gift. He had a progressive and unique way to solve problems. He drew up diagrams of how to build a new kind of foundation for our home that would keep out the cold.

Everything was normal and then it wasn't. Jewish families began to close up their homes and leave to go live with family in remote areas of the country. Our mother wanted us to do the same thing. But Marius' wife didn't want to leave her family and David had exams he was preparing for. Life went on as it always does on the outside, one day after another, sometimes sunny, sometimes rainy and cold. But inside our homes we whispered and wondered if what we were hearing was true.

"What were you hearing, Grand Pop?" He had stopped speaking and was twisting his hands together over and over in his lap. I lean forward and touch my grandfather's fingers to stop him from hurting his hands. I glance at Elizabeth and see her face, silent and silvery in the moonlight. Grand Pop clears his throat again and keeps telling us his story.

And then, one day, all of our lives changed in five minutes. Trucks rumbled into our small village and soldiers in uniforms flowed through the streets like a soup of pure gray terror. They came with their flags, their sharp voices, and their guns. They lined up people and simply . . . killed them.

Elizabeth cried out some word in Spanish I didn't understand and began to cry. She wiped her eyes fiercely. Grand Pop reached over and squeezed her hand.

It just happened so fast. Then they made me and David pick up our parents' bodies and carry them to a grave they'd dug for all the people they'd killed. Marius was there, staring into the big hole where he'd just put his wife. I will never forget the way the people's bodies were tossed like dominoes, twisted and turned into a pile of upside down, sideways lumps of clay, objects that seemed unreal. An unforgettable vision.

I was too stunned to say or do anything. The idea of anyone shooting my parents and making me and Jared carry their bodies was too awful to think about. I could never, ever think about that. But here it was anyway, and it was me who reached out to squeeze Grand Pop's other hand and that's how we sat; me, Elizabeth, and Grand Pop gripping each other's hands, crying, my heart thumping in fear of what will come next as Grand Pop kept going with this horrible story. Which wasn't even a story, but his very own life.

I could tell he didn't tell this story often. Maybe never. His voice was ragged and torn like he as searching for words.

The soldiers grabbed me, David, and Marius and dragged us onto a truck with others from the village. It was a long journey, full of dust with no water or food. They treated us as if we were animals who had already died.

Grand Pop cleared his throat. I know that this is the story Mommy didn't want me to hear. But it had happened to Grand Pop. Just like September 11, had happened to us. I couldn't just close my ears and not listen.

For one year, we lived in a camp, me, David and Marius. It never once occurred to me that I wouldn't live, or that my brothers wouldn't survive with me. I didn't fear the soldiers or their evil. I kept it outside of me, never letting it touch me. Until one day.

Elizabeth gripped my hand tightly.

David was using his genius mind to figure out ways to get us out of there. Marius and I and a few others helped him get whatever he needed. David measured and tapped walls and made holes in the ground and drew diagrams in his mind. But he wouldn't take the chance of writing anything down. Instead, he whispered these diagrams over and over to me so that I would memorize them. He would say, "Oscar, remember that at the edge of bunk 29, the wall turns at a 90 degree angle. Okay? Do not forget."

It was not until later that I realized what David was doing. He didn't need to tell me the calculations so he could remember them — he already knew them. He had the magic of a perfect memory.

Jared has that, too, I thought. He remembers every single thing he reads. Jared is like David.

David was telling me about it all in case something happened to him. Our escape plan was David's purpose in life. He told me it would be his life's work. To save our family name. To save our future, our people, who had not been born as yet, but was already part of us.

Like me and Jared and Mommy, I thought.

And one day, we did escape. Me and Marius. We escaped exactly as David had plotted and planned.

Grand Pop sat back on his rock and spread his hands open. "And here I am."

"What about David?" Elizabeth and I both asked at the same time.

"And Marius?" I asked. "He's Mommy's uncle, right? And mine, too."

Grand Pop's voice drops so low I can barely hear him.

The Nazi soldiers killed David one day for no reason at all. Marius and I saw it and if it weren't for people holding us back, me and Marius would have died too because we struggled to run and grab that soldier and kill him ourselves. We would have been killers just like him.

My body is trembling so much I can't stop it. I'm shaking and shaking as if this is happening to me. Maybe it is. Maybe I'm the one watching my brother die and I can't do anything to stop it. I look up at the sky. No stars, no moon, no comets or planes flying high, just pure black the way the sky is sometimes.

The day after David died, Marius and I escaped following the exact plan David had plotted. We ran at night, hid during the day in barns and under farming equipment and in sheds and behind trees. It was summertime and we were forest boys, so we knew what to do although there were times I didn't think I could go on just thinking about David. But I had to for Marius. We finally ended up in Denmark.

We heard about ships that would take us to an island in the Caribbean Sea, Hispaniola, now the Republica Dominicana, which was offering a safe haven for Jewish refugees. Marius and I applied. I'll never forget that other journey and leaving our homes forever.

Grand Pop's voice got real sad, as if the worse part of this story was still to come. I didn't think I could take any more.

We arrived here in 1945. It was so hot, like fire burning our skin. There were about 500 of us. The first thing we built was a synagogue, and gave thanks and praise for our escape.

"But what happened to Marius?" I ask.

Marius made it here, but only in his body. He left his heart and mind back there. He could never stop living the memories, could never live a new life. Marius died the same time as David. He completely stopped speaking.

I am shaking even more, and I wrap my arms around my body. Grand Pop has tears on his face as he goes on.

I did everything I could to help him. I showed him rainbows. I took him to the beach. I gave him orchids. I saved money and went to Santo Domingo to buy a small piano and brought it back for him. Nothing worked. He refused to play the piano. He refused to see anything good again.

"But you were happy again?" Elizabeth asks.

Grand Pop shook his head. "Marius' unhappiness became

mine too. It took a long time for me to start living my own life. Now, I'm happy at the small things. Like watching birds. Or reading a good book. Or eating a delicious meal. I never look for happiness in anything big. I can only be happy in small doses."

"Like medicine?"

"Exactly," he says. "Happiness is a dose of medicine I take every day, always.

"Did Marius ever speak again?" Elizabeth asks. I know she's thinking of her Mamí with her sad, staring eyes.

"Only a little. He talked of the horrors of the camp, of David's death, and of our escape. That was all he ever spoke about. That one year of horror and sadness became his entire life. I told him that we could start new lives, learn new things, make friends, have a new family here or in Canada if he wanted to move. But he said no. What was the point of trying when it could all be taken away so easily, so quickly. It was Marius' decision to stop hoping. And finally, I had to realize that nothing I could do would make him happy. There was absolutely nothing I could do about it."

Elizabeth and I look at each other. Tears are streaming down her face into her hair. I'm wiping my own eyes with the backs of my hands. Grand Pop looks at the two of us. He shakes his head, and reaches out and takes our hands into his own strong ones again.

"I'm not telling you this to make you sad," he says. "I'm telling you so you can know why."

"Know why what?" Elizabeth asks.

"Why you are not responsible if someone isn't happy. Even the people you love the most in the world."

"That's what Jared said." Elizabeth says.

"But where is Marius, now?" I ask fearfully.

Grand Pop shakes his head. "I wasn't planning to go this far into the story of my life. But okay, Marius ended up in a hospital for the last twenty years of his life. I visited him almost every day. At the very end, he started playing the piano again. The same songs he used to play for our mother and father in our village in Germany."

Grand Pop holds up his hands, "Okay, that's enough. No more questions." He reaches over and ruffles my hair. He pulls one of Elizabeth's long curls. We are both sitting there with not a word between us.

"I do think about David every day though," says Grand Pop, suddenly. "He's the reason I got to start my life over. I think about him all the time."

The moon slips out from behind a cloud all of a sudden as if David heard us. Me, Elizabeth, and Grand Pop stare at the moonlight shining in a straight bright path, a road across the water. The stars emerge from the black sky. I feel the stars and the sea and the moon right inside me as if they are me and I'm them.

Funny how Grand Pop ended up on a Caribbean island after his horrible time, and now I am here, too. Both of us living next to the sea that never ends, finding a new life to live, with sadness surrounding us.

Then, as I gaze out at that sea and think about Grand Pop's journey, I feel like Uncle David is here too. And I smile.

"You and Jared are the family David wanted me to carry on. You are your Uncle David's purpose. His legacy." Grand Pop speaks directly to me.

I have no idea what a legacy is but I remember the priest back in New York talking about our purpose in life. I am Uncle David's purpose.

I look at the moon. "Hello to you, Uncle David," I say in my mind. "Look at me, sitting here with your brother, Oscar. My Grand Pop. Your legacy."

25

brandt
THINKING AND THINKING AND THINKING ...

OW THAT WE WERE no longer planning how to make our mothers happy, Elizabeth and I spend most of our free time with Grand Pop in his garden courtyard, also known as the den of contemplation. Grand Pop reads. Elizabeth makes sea shell necklaces to sell at the beach to help her Mamí with expenses. And I just sit, thinking and thinking. Jared joins us sometimes, playing his Gameboy or reading, and once in a while talking to Elizabeth. Only Elizabeth. Their voices join together like my favourite song.

One day, out of the blue, Elizabeth says to Grand Pop. "Maybe you should come over and meet Doña Maria."

"Why is that, Miss Elizabeth?" he asks. Grand Pop has gotten in the habit of calling her "Miss Elizabeth", and he calls me "Mister Brandt." He calls Jared, "J-Man." We all like our nicknames.

Elizabeth shrugs. "I think Doña Maria is sad and trying to swim out of a deep hole. She just needs some help. Maybe a new friend."

Grand Pop blinks. "I used to know Doña Maria many years ago."

"Really?" asks Elizabeth, looking up from the floor where she is leaning on her elbows stringing sea shells.

Grand Pop smiles. "Oh yes, we were sweethearts once."

"WHAT!" Elizabeth leaps up from the floor. Grand Pop

grins and I can see the lines around his eyes and on his forehead wiggling about like dashes of light.

"Tell us," begs Elizabeth, but my grandfather shakes his head no. "Another time, another place," he says. "But I'll tell you one thing, she left me for that sea captain and it broke my heart."

Elizabeth and I stare at each other. My grandfather was full of surprises.

"Well, love never dies," says Elizabeth.

Grand Pop nods. "No, it never does."

And with that, we all feel better. No, love doesn't die. It may be buried a bit, it may change form, but true love is always there. At least that is what Elizabeth and I decide the next morning as we walk to Sosúa Beach. And before I know it, Elizabeth has a new mission. To get Grand Pop and Doña Maria back together again.

"You think it will work?" I ask.

"Of course, it will," she declares. "It will be my Master Grand Plan."

I didn't say anything then to discourage her. Because I, too, was thinking about a plan.

Several nights after I'd heard Grand Pop's story, I laid in bed for a long time thinking about the terrible things that people do to each other. I had seen real-life images on TV. I'd heard about the killings and bombings from Mommy. And magazine articles and newspapers blared out destruction everywhere. And now Grand Pop's story was like lightening striking me through my heart.

I rolled over and got out of bed and went to lean on the windowsill.

"What's wrong?"

I looked over at Jared. He was sitting up in his bed.

"I don't know," I whispered.

"Go back to bed, then."

"I can't sleep. I'm scared."

"Of what? Stop being a baby."

I didn't answer. I was scared. Or maybe sad. I didn't even know.

"Did something happen?" Jared asked, quietly.

"No," I lied.

Jared snapped his fingers. "Get with the program, Brandt," he said. "Don't lie to me."

I didn't say anything.

"So, what is it this time? The mermaid girl wants you to dance under the full moon with mermaid pearls around your neck?"

I couldn't help but giggle. I climbed back into bed. "Don't talk about Elizabeth like that."

"You know she's crazy, right?"

"No, she isn't."

"Of course she is. She thinks she's really a mermaid."

"I know," I said.

Jared waited a moment. "You don't actually believe her, do you?"

"I thought about it."

"You have to think about it?" he asked, incredulously.

"Well, if she is a mermaid, does it matter?"

"Duh! If she's a mermaid then, she's not human. Earth to Brandt … not human, that means, alien being …."

"Elizabeth is not an alien," I giggled for real that time. "I mean mermaids are not aliens. They're fish."

Even in the darkness I could see Jared roll his eyes. It was in the way he shook his head.

"Next thing, you will be telling me that you're Batman."

I giggled and threw a pillow at Jared.

He threw it back at me. "Well, she is pretty like a mermaid," I snapped at him.

"Hmmmmm," said Jared. And then he rolled over and went to sleep.

But I didn't go right to sleep. Instead, I lay with my head on my hands and thought about everything Grand Pop had said. I thought about Uncle David and his Plan of escape and his hope and his love for his brothers. Uncle David had a grand Plan and because of it, I am here alive and breathing in Sosúa. His Plan could not be for nothing. It couldn't be for Mommy to end up sad and lonely. Or for Jared to be angry and unhappy. Uncle David did not devise his great Plan for that!

I thought about my Uncle David until the sky got lighter and my mind was swirling again, but not with sadness. With something else. Something that was making me think very hard.

26

elizabeth
YOU HAVE TO BELIEVE

BRANDT AND I WALK TO Sosúa Beach carrying empanadas and pineapple juice in a back pack. He's quiet and looks as if he's thinking of something far from here. I have to snap my fingers in front his face a few times to get his attention.

"What?" he asks, absentmindedly.

"Pay attention, Brandt, I need your help."

Brandt smiles at me and I can't be mad at him.

"Okay, we have to get Doña Maria and Señor Oscar together again."

Brandt looks skeptical.

"It's LOVE, Brandt," I say, a little dramatically, but I have to make my point because he's not getting as excited as I feel.

"Love?" he asks.

"Yes, love," I reply, "Love solves every problem in this world."

"Really?"

"Yes," I say, although how do I know. "It causes some problems too," I add, thinking that Jared looks at me like I'm a leper.

"Well, if love solves everything, why don't we get my mother to fall in love with someone, too?"

I stop dead in my tracks. "Brandt, you're a genius!"

He looks puzzled. Then he breaks into a big smile. "A genius like Uncle David?"

I can't speak. The look in Brandt's eyes is pure hope.

"Brandt, what are you thinking of?"

He shakes his head. "I'm thinking Uncle David is here with us."

I look around. "Here?" I ask.

"He is, you know."

The way he says it so sure and certain make the hair on my arms stand up. It's how I feel about Papí.

"I don't doubt it, Brandt. But how do you know?"

"Because I can feel him."

"Oh," I say. "I can feel my Papí here, too." I smile at Brandt. Maybe one day I'll show him the menu and tell him about my dreams of being trapped with Papí. It was too spooky for poor Clara, who I hardly saw anymore after I missed so much school and had to go back one grade. I didn't mind. Missing a grade meant nothing at all.

We continue walking down the beach. "Okay, I think we should introduce your mother to my Tío Franco." I clap my hands. "It's the perfect solution. They are the same age and he likes really smart girls."

"How do you know that?"

"Cause he likes me, silly."

Brandt laughs out loud.

"What's so funny?" I demand. "You know someone better for her to fall in love with?

"Elizabeth, if we can't make people happy, like Grand Pop and

Jared said, I'm not sure we can make them fall in love, either."

I think about that for a minute. "You have to believe," I say. "It's like making a perfect flan. You need all the right ingredients and if you miss just one — like the sweet condensed milk, it won't work."

"You're making me hungry," says Brandt.

We settle under a coconut tree and open up our picnic. I hand out the salt fish empanadas and they are so good, we stop talking for a while.

"So, can you make a flan?" asks Brandt.

"Of course."

"Well, let's make a flan and we will give some to your Doña Maria and some to Grandfather and some to Tío Franco and some to Mommy."

I nod. "And then what?"

Brandt shrugs his shoulders. "You have to believe, remember?"

"Yes, Brandt," I smile back at him, co-conspirators to the end. "You have to believe."

27

elizabeth

EVERYTHING IS BETTER WITH FOOD

RANDT COMES WITH ME to my house and we start the flan. We gather all the ingredients – the can of sweetened condensed milk, the evaporated milk, and six eggs that we carry carefully out of the icebox.

"We also need some coconut milk," I say. Brandt searches the cupboards and finally finds a can of coconut milk.

"I thought I would have to go climb that coconut tree out there," he laughs.

I giggle, "Do you even know which coconuts have milk and which ones are old and dried up?"

Brandt looks outside at the trees waving their green palm fronds in the breeze. "Nope," he says. "I'm from New York City!" He sounds so funny that I bend over laughing as I beat the eggs.

"So, it's a good thing we have this can here," I say, and shake the can around.

As I turn on the oven and caramelize the pan for the flan, I wonder about this crazy idea.

"Well, if it doesn't work," says Brandt, reading my mind as usual, "we'll still have good food to eat."

He has a point. Flan is my favourite thing to eat. And it's so smooth and creamy and delicious that anyone could fall in love just taking one bite. I don't tell Brandt that I want to give Jared a piece of the flan, too. I'm not in love with Jared or anything, but still. As I whisk the ingredients together, I smile to myself. I see Jared's smile, his hands counting out sea shells for my necklaces. I hear his voice, deep and sure as he reads aloud some funny parts of his books, jokes I don't always get but I laugh anyway because he's telling it to me. Being around Jared is different than being with Brandt. With Jared, it's all about being my best self. With Brandt, I'm just my real self. I wish my real self was my best self but it isn't. Not yet.

Meanwhile, Brandt and I try hard not to make a mess for Mamí. During the stirring of the eggs and the condensed milk, Doña Maria walks in. I try to hide what we are making but she sniffs the air and says happily, "Is that flan, Elizabeth?"

I nod and she kisses me on my forehead. "I can't wait to try it, mi amor."

Brandt and I look at each other as soon as she walks out and we burst into laughter. "See, it's working already," I tell him.

Brandt holds the strainer while I tiptoe and pour the mixture through the strainer into the pan. Then we place the pan with the flan mixture into a bigger pan and pour water around it. Our flan is now sitting like a sailing ship in the middle of a sea. We place the pans into the oven and close the oven door.

"There!"

"What now?" asks Brandt.

"We clean up."

Brandt and I wash the bowls and spoons and wipe down the counter then we sit on the back steps next to the pool of sparkling sea water that rushes in and out of the rocks.

Brandt is humming and I'm making funny faces in the sand with a stick.

"So, how should we give them the flan?" I ask Brandt.

He keeps on humming. The thing with Brandt is I just sit there and wait and he eventually tells me whatever he has to tell me when he's ready.

"A poem," he finally says.

"What?" I ask. I'm not sure I heard him correctly.

"We will give them a poem and a piece of flan."

"A poem?"

"Yes," says Brandt. "People fall in love in poems."

"Really? That's news to me." I don't know any poems.

"My mother reads me poems all the time at night before I go to sleep. Before we moved here, I mean."

I look at him amazed.

"Yes, and a lot of them were about love. Although my favourite one was about a barefoot boy."

I stare at Brandt. A barefoot boy? Was he making this up?

"I don't know any poems," I finally admit.

"Yes, you do."

"No," I whisper. "I really don't."

"All you have to do is feel something very strongly in your heart and then write down what you feel. That'll be your poem."

I frown. "It's that easy?"

"Yes. That's how you write a poem."

"Okay," I say. "I'll give it a try."

Brandt smiles. "You always speak as if you're saying a poem."

"Really, like when? Like now?"

Brandt laughs. "No, not now. But a lot of times you tell me about fairy wings and mermaids dancing and it sounds like a poem."

I smile. If Brandt thinks I can write a poem, well, then, I will write one.

I smell the flan cooking and the burnt sugar and coconut are mixing together into a wonderful scent.

I want to work on my poem right away so I go inside and leave Brandt sitting by the yellow tree looking at the little pool.

"I'll be back. I'm going to write a poem."

28

brandt
AND THEN THERE'S THE PLAN ...

WHILE ELIZABETH WRITES her poem, I sit on the rocks and watch the water swirl around my bare feet. I watch the sunlight playing games of tic tac toe on the water's surface. My eyes are focused on the back and forth swaying of the small wavelets.

Soon, my eyes are closing down and instead of the water I'm seeing myself pressing my face against the window of the Tower watching the world far below. I see Señor Hernandez carrying a cake. I see Jared pulling me out of a smoky church. I see him giving me his headphones to listen to my *Grease* songs. I see Mommy sitting and crying in Burger King behind a newspaper with large headlines. I see Jared smashing a vase of moonbeams and Mommy holding onto a telephone asking for someone to do something about my brother.

Through it all, I hear Father Eugene's words from his sermon as clear as day. "God has a plan for each of us. A special plan for your life."

What if my plan is to get Mommy and Jared to stop hovering around each other like static balloons that give off electrical charges whenever they touch? I hate being the one in the middle, feeling like I have to choose a side when there are no sides to choose. I want us to be a family, a happy family, who talk to each other and love each other and stand together through anything.

Like Uncle David died for.

A plan is forming in my mind slowly like a picture drawn with invisible ink - I know it's there, I just can't quite see it as yet. I don't have Jared's Amazing Brain to figure it out. I don't have Elizabeth's strong faith in wild ideas. All I have is my hope to try and make this plan work. This plan that started way back before I was born. Before Jared was born, and even before Mommy was born.

29

elizabeth

THE POEM

SIT AT THE KITCHEN TABLE and bite the end of my pencil. My brain is a frozen lake.

Okay, Brandt said I have to feel strongly – I shut my eyes and concentrate very hard. But nothing comes out my pencil.

The flan is all finished and I take it out of the oven and put it on the stove top to cool down. Brandt leaves for home and I still sit there concentrating.

Writing a poem is hard.

I close my eyes and press my fingertips over my eyes to keep the bright sunlight out. I can see sparkles inside my eyelids. They are a kaleidoscope of colours and images. Beautiful red and yellow colours. Dancing, flickering inside my eyelids. All of that hidden until you close your eyes. It's right there all the time but sometimes you have to see with more than your eyes.

Like with Jared. If you just look at how he acts or listen to his words you miss the biggest and best part of him. He's ALWAYS there. By Brandt's side. By his mother's. By my side, too, helping with necklaces he probably couldn't care less about, but still there beside me. Jared sticks with you. That's his love.

And that's when I open my eyes and write:

Your love cannot be seen
With a smile or kiss or touch

It beams upon me
Surrounding me, feeding me
in a grand moment of perfection.

That's it – that's my poem. I laugh. Next, I write a poem
about my flan.

Sugar sweet
creamy full
smooth as sliver nights.
Flan is warm rain
dancing drops
misty days and
kissing smiles.
Slow and cool
like blue-black stars
shaky as a map
sealed with
Mamí and Papí's
hearts
perfect for all time.

I'm so happy that I get up and twirl around the kitchen singing
and flinging my kitchen cloth here and there as if it is a fairy wand.
Mamí walks in just then. "What are you doing, hija?"
"Mamí, I wrote a poem. Two poems! And I made a flan."
Mamí looks at my flan on the stove. "Looks good," she says
sniffing the pan. "But why are you dancing?" Then she holds up

her hands. "Don't tell me, it's the mermaid's birthday?"

"Mamí, don't be silly," I laugh. "That was two weeks ago, remember?"

And then Mamí laughs. She really laughs. I stop in mid-spin. "Mamí, you're laughing," I say.

"Yes, because you are a funny little girl," she replies.

Without even thinking twice I rush over to Mamí and throw my arms around her neck. "Mamí, I'm sorry. I'm so sorry about Papí. I miss him so much."

"Oh Elizabeth." Mamí wraps her arms around me. "It's not for you to be sorry. You are my joy. You're the only reason I get up and keep going during this bad time."

I step back and look up into Mamí's eyes. They are still sad, but also smiling at me in a way I never noticed before.

"You're my life, Elizabeth."

Now it's me who's crying.

"So, are you going to read your poems to me, or do I have to wait until I eat this flan?"

I wipe away my tears quickly and pick up my newly written poems still ink wet on the paper. As I read my poems out loud to Mamí, I read them to Papí also in my head. I love you, Papí, I say to him silently when I finish reading the poems.

Mamí is smiling and wiping her eyes and tells me I must keep writing more poems.

That's when I understand that being happy all by yourself can rub off on people. It's that simple.

30

brandt
THERE IS HOPE

NE SUNNY MORNING, I'm thinking about what Elizabeth told me. How she was happy all by herself and her mother joined in, unplanned and unexpected just like magic. I walk onto the balcony where Mommy is sitting with a magazine in her lap. It has a picture of the Twin Towers on it and huge headlines in red writing about September 11. Mommy is talking on the telephone to someone in New York because she's saying, "Well, down here, we don't have to worry about that. Down here, there are no subways or bridges so we don't have to worry about bomb threats."

I feel for the first time that there is no way I can get Mommy to forget this horrible thing that turned her life upside down. It is and always will be part of her. So, I wait until she finishes with her call.

"Hi Mommy," I say, sitting next to her.

"Hi sweetie," she says back. "You need something?" Her eyes look red and sad as usual.

I hesitate. I look out over the sea. Ripples of currents move beneath the surface. I wonder if I will ever get used to seeing the galloping waves. I think about Robin Hood and his brown horse. How happy he looked dashing about the forest on his horse and sorting out all sorts of dilemmas while perched high up. He reminds me of Elizabeth, with her cheerful, hopeful face dreaming of crazy things like searching for mermaid treasure at the bottom of the sea. Robin Hood and Elizabeth are the same, both believing the best of everyone and never giving up.

As I stare at the waves leaping about, I wonder what it would be like to have fun like Robin Hood, riding a horse and helping people at the same time. Since we moved to Sosúa I've seen horses on the beach, but I never thought of riding one. Until now.

"Have you ever ridden a horse?" I ask.

Mommy looks at me a little strangely. "A horse?"

I realize that it is exactly what I would love to do in this new place. "Yes, a horse, you ever rode a horse?"

Mommy scrunches up her forehead thinking, "No, Brandt, I never rode a horse, why?"

"Well, there's a place called Gypsy Ranch between Sosúa and Cabarete and they have horses to ride. We can rent them."

"You mean you and Jared want to ride horses?" Mommy looks interested in something for the first time in a long time.

"No, I want to ride a horse."

Mommy screws up her nose. "Well I don't know if I . . ."

"It's on the beach. You and Jared can come, too." I don't say I hope they don't spoil my fun but that's what I'm thinking.

"We can ride up and down the beach. If you fall off, you fall in the waves. And since we are living in a new place, I thought we should try new things." Boy, I was sounding like a commercial.

"Does Jared want to do this?" Her forehead is still scrunched up.

"Yes," I say, even though I haven't spoken to Jared about any horses as yet. But I know I can convince him to ride one.

"Well, I don't see why we can't give it a try," says Mommy.

"Yipeee," I say, and I give her a hug and a kiss. "Can we do it tomorrow?"

Mommy looks surprised, but she doesn't say no. "We'll see," she says. "You want to invite Elizabeth?"

I shake my head. "No, just us three."

"Okay," says Mommy. "I'll call the ranch and make reservations." She picks up the phone and I go to look for Jared.

He's sitting on his bed playing with his new video game. I sit down next to him and watch as he fights aliens. One thing I've learned about Mommy and Jared. You can't just walk up to them and start talking. They live so much in their minds that I end up upsetting whatever they were thinking about and then they snap at me. So, the best thing is to just sit there for a few minutes and wait. It's as if they have to process me being there, like a computer program. After awhile, I say, "Jared, guess what?"

He keeps looking at the screen and punching the controls on the handset. "What?"

"We are going to ride horses tomorrow."

He glances over at me quickly then back at the screen again. "We are?"

"Yes," I say, nodding my head up and down, so he can see the big Yes. "You, me and Mommy."

"Mommy is going to ride a horse?" he snorts.

"Yup," I answer.

"I don't know how to ride a horse."

"Neither does Mommy."

"Oh," says Jared. "Well, then, why are we going to ride these horses?"

"Because."

"Because why?"

"Because it'll be fun - it's on the beach and we're going to ride in the waves."

"Okay," shrugs Jared. "If you say so."

"And Mommy wants to ride a horse. And she wants us to ride with her."

Jared put down the controls. He raises one eyebrow at me the way the Rock does right before he wrestles. "I get it. I get it. We're riding horses."

I laugh. "I can't do that. How do you do that?"

I jump up to look in the mirror as I try my best to squinch up one eyebrow while keeping the other one down.

Jared laughs and walks over to the mirror. "It's muscle control. You have to think about it and concentrate."

I try again.

"No, silly, not like that," says Jared, as I try my best to copy him.

Finally, I just take one hand and hold down one of my eyebrows while I wiggle the other one up and down. "See? I'm doing it."

Jared cracks up laughing and we fall back on the beds. Well, he wasn't talking much but at least he was laughing again. The thing with Jared, or anyone I suppose, is that you have to do stuff they like. You can't just always do stuff you like and expect them to have fun with you. And that is Mommy's and Jared's mistake. They both like such different things that they can never play with each other. Like Mommy hates video games. But Mommy likes to read all the time. And Jared likes to read, but he reads books that Mommy doesn't like, such as science fiction or fantasy.

Me, I do stuff everyone likes. I read poems with Mommy and I play video games with Jared. I make flan with Elizabeth or sit and talk with Grand Pop. I just like doing stuff with them and it doesn't really matter what it is they want to do. But now, I think I have found something that I want to do myself, and maybe Jared and Mommy will both like it too . Who knows?

The plan, which has formed like magic in my mind, is to get them both doing the same fun thing. Something that neither one of them knows how to do already. So, they can learn it together. It's a simple plan. But I hope it works.

And in a way, it's just like making delicious flan to help people fall in love. You don't know if it'll work, but you have to start somewhere.

31

elizabeth
LOVE AND FLAN AND FRIENDS

HERE'S ONLY ONE THING to do when you find out your new best friend is going horse back riding with his mother and the boy you like. You invite yourself along even if you've never ridden a horse in your life. In fact, you're so deathly afraid of horses that you also invite your mother, who is smiling in bits and pieces, as if, like Señor Oscar, she can only trust happiness in small doses.

Then, your mother helps you pack up the love flan and when your Doña Maria asks if she can come along, too, you say, sure, it's a family outing. Then you call your best friend and say, "Make sure your grandfather is coming, too."

And then, when Tío Franco just happens to show up on the very same morning of the horse back riding outing, you throw up your hands and leave the rest up to fate and destiny. And flan!

32

brandt

AND FINALLY, THERE IS JOY ...

IKE ALL SIMPLE PLANS, my idea of riding horses does not stay simple at all. Instead, it snowballs into a huge adventure. By the next morning, every one who has heard even a whisper about the plan, wants to join in. So, by ten o' clock the next day, our garden is filled with people who want to try riding horses. And that's when I realize that my little idea to try riding a horse is turning out to be a big opportunity to cast our love wish over everyone.

There is Grand Pop and Doña Maria, and Mommy and Jared, and Mommy's sister, Auntie Sonia, who lives in the north coast town of Samana, and is a yoga instructor. She arrived yesterday to spend time with us.

Elizabeth's uncle, Tío Franco, the artist from Moca, is there too. All of these people converging on us at the same time cannot be a coincidence. Converge and coincidence are my new words. They mean uniting and chance. And it's exactly what I'm doing; taking a chance uniting Jared and Mommy.

Elizabeth comes excitedly clutching Doña Maria's hand, and Elizabeth's Mamí comes as we are all piling into a specially hired taxi van. She runs up our hill with a basket that looks as if it's full of food and snacks. And hopefully some flan.

"Mamí, you going to ride a horse, too?" Elizabeth's eyes are shining with hope.

Her mother nods. Her face is flushed from running up the hill and her eyes are bright. "Yes, mi amor, I love horses, we rode them all the time in the countryside where I grew up."

"She means in Moca," says Tío Franco to Grand Pop and Mommy.

We all squish together to make room for Elizabeth's Mamí and off we go down the hill and along the seaside road to Cabarete. I look around the taxi van and see that Mommy is talking to Elizabeth's Mamí in lightning fast Spanish in the front seat. Grand Pop is leaning close to Doña Maria pointing at the passing scenery.

Elizabeth is busy chatting and laughing with Jared. Tío Franco is holding Auntie Sonia by her elbow so she won't fall off the edge of the seat. Okay, things are not going according to plan here. Mommy should be sitting next to Jared. Or even Tío Franco. But instead, the two mothers are busy talking about who knows what? Every once in a while, Mommy glances at me and I begin to wonder what I have done.

When we arrive at the Gypsy Ranch, I climb out of the back of the van and there is a ring of horses just like in books. A corral it's called. I know that word. There are three brown horses, a black one, a white one, and two gray horses. And right behind them all are two beautiful, golden brown and white horses with long, swishing yellow tails. Wow! I have never been so close to a horse before. They already have on saddles and blankets and things to put your feet in. Stirrups, I think. A boy about Jared's age is strapping horse gear onto the two golden horses.

For the first time that day, we all are silent. Then, Mommy and Elizabeth's Mamí begin whispering to each other and pointing at me.

"Oh oh."

Jared is nudging Elizabeth and pointing at the horse he wants to ride.

"This one is Fuego," says the boy, brushing the horse Jared has pointed to.

"It means "Fire" in English," says Mommy to Jared and she smiles at him. "You think you can handle that?"

Jared nods, and smiles back. "I think so."

Okay, plan in action. Mommy and Jared are converging.

There's a lot of giggling as we all try to find the right horse for ourselves.

"I want a small, quiet horse," Mommy says, pointing at one of the small gray horses.

"Not me," says Elizabeth's Mamí. "I want one with some real thunder in its hooves."

The stable boy laughs. "We have one called Hurricane."

"Perfect!" says Mamí. Mamí's name is Lourdes, but she said Jared and I could call her Mamí, so we do.

Tío Franco and Auntie Sonia are huddled together pointing and laughing.

"Well, all I want is an obedient horse," Auntie Sonia giggles.

Tío Franco snorts. "Yes, for now. But that can get boring." And the two of them elbow each other and laugh.

Elizabeth stands back. "I don't think I want to ride a horse at all," she whispers.

"Oh, baby, of course you will ride a horse. You are mi hija!" says Mamí.

Elizabeth looks doubtful. "I could wait here with the food and drinks," she offers.

Mamí looks like she's thinking about it, when Jared steps in. "It'll be okay, Elizabeth. Ride next to me, we can master this thing together."

My eyebrows shoot up - both of them in a perfect Rock imitation. This plan was going in all different directions. Mommy and Jared are supposed to learn to ride together. But Mommy is busy getting riding tips from Mamí Lourdes, and Jared and Elizabeth look inseparable. As for Tío Franco, he's so busy laughing and talking to Auntie Sonia that he hasn't even noticed my mother, although they are the ones who're supposed to fall in love. The only thing working out is that Doña Maria and Grand Pop are practically holding hands.

"Can you ride a horse, Señor Oscar?" asks Doña Maria.

"Sí, Doña Maria. I have ridden horses in Germany with my brothers through the Black Forest."

Mommy looks over at her father. "Really, Papa, I didn't know that."

Grand Pop nods. "It's true."

"You never talked about that before," Mommy says.

"I know," says Grand Pop. "Maybe it's time to start talking more about my brothers, Marius and David." He winks at me.

I wink back at Grand Pop.

In the end, it's the Gypsy Ranch owners, Señor and Señora Mendoza who assign the horses to us based on our riding experience. I want one of the golden brown horses with the yellow tails, but I don't say anything. I just keep hoping.

Finally, everyone is sitting high up above the ground on their horses. Everyone except for me. Mamí Lourdes is on Hurricane. Mommy is on a gray mare called Loopy. We all laugh at that name and Mommy says she hopes she won't be loopy by the end of the ride.

Jared is on Fuego and Elizabeth is on a small, yellow Pikachu-looking horse called Pikachu. Jared, Elizabeth and I giggle at the name and Jared says, "Don't worry, little Pika, Ash is right here."

I can't believe how gentle Jared is speaking to Elizabeth. And he had scoffed about her being a mermaid. To tell the truth, it looks as if Elizabeth has forgotten all about her plan to make Doña Maria and Grand Pop fall in love. All of her attention is on Jared, and he seems fine with that.

Tío Franco helps Auntie Sonia up on her horse. It's one of the lovely golden brown horses, whose name is Honey. Tío Franco and Auntie Sonia are staring in each other's eyes and anyone could see that Tío Franco is already falling in love with Mommy's sister.

Mamí Lourdes and Mommy are looking at them and giggling behind their hands like the girls at school. Auntie Sonia even blushes when Tío Franco pats her horse and then swings himself up on a tall, black and white, wild-looking horse called Tornado. He looks like he rides horses every day. Tío Franco looks like a real Dominican cowboy.

And then finally, they pick a horse for me. The moment I see my horse, I smile. I hadn't seen him in the corral nuzzling about with the others. This horse is sleek with neat, pointed ears that flicker back and forth, and he looks at me with a steady gaze. He is mostly white with brown speckles along his legs. The horse nods at me and I nod back. It's like we are both saying "Hello" to each other.

I touch my horse on his neck and smooth his hairs gently. Mr. Mendoza tells me his name is Amigo – which means "friend."

"Perfect," I whisper to him.

Amigo nods his sleek head again.

"Okay, Amigo," I say to my horse. "We got things to do."

Mr. Mendoza hoists me up and over onto Amigo's back and I'm sitting tall like everyone else. The ground is far below and looks a little scary as soon as Amigo begins swaying down the road and I slide from side to side. I can hear Elizabeth squealing as her horse follows mine onto the road that leads to the beach. After we weave in and out between trees, bushes and over fallen coconuts, there before us is the blue Caribbean Sea. The sand is a buttery yellow that glows under Amigo's hooves. Amigo tosses his head and neighs.

"Easy, Amigo," I whisper. Off we go, me and Amigo, trotting down the beach, through the waves, splashing up water left and right. I can hear Mommy and Grand Pop and Jared and everyone else laughing and shouting. But all I can think about is holding on for my life. This great plan has come down to one thing and one thing only – not falling off my horse and into the water, which looks like it's a mile below me.

I want to look around and see how everyone is doing but I don't dare take my eyes off Amigo. I hear Grandfather saying something about the lush green hills where the movie Jurassic Park was filmed. Out of the corners of my eyes, I see ghostly mist rising above dark green mountains off to my left that looks just like the scenes in the movie.

But Amigo does not have time for sightseeing. He wants to move. I struggle to hold on. Together, we bump up and down and I grip his body tight with my legs. The salty sea water splashes into my mouth and wets my face. My clothes are getting sandy from Grand Pop's horse kicking sand back on me and Amigo.

Mommy goes trotting by on her little gray horse, Loopy, and Jared is right next to her on Fuego, laughing and shouting, "Are you okay, Mommy?"

Mommy is shaking her head and laughing, too. "I don't know. I think so."

"Hold on tight, Mommy," he shouts, as Fuego dashes off and Jared screams. Mamí Lourdes and Tío Franco fly by in a whirl on Hurricane and Tornado. They are brother and sister, whooping and racing each other down the curving beach, like they are little kids again.

Doña Maria is trotting slowly with Auntie Sonia while Grand Pop keeps circling back around to check on them. Every few minutes, Tío Franco looks back and waves at Auntie Sonia and once she shouts out, "Don't fall!" She could have been speaking to any one of us, but we all know who she really meant, as Tío Franco dashes up the beach in a blaze toward her.

Elizabeth stays near me, her Pikachu side by side with Amigo.

"It's like writing a poem," she shouts over the sea and sand and screams and shouts of our families.

"What?" I shout back, staring down at how Amigo's legs are dancing between the shallow breaking waves.

"Riding a horse is like writing a poem. It comes to you after a while."

"Oh, okay," I say.

Elizabeth giggles. "Like falling in love. Or making a flan."

"Like being happy," I shout back.

"Yup," she agrees, as Pikachu tosses water high up onto both of us. Amigo shakes his head and tosses some back.

"Cool it," I tell him.

Amigo flickers his ears at me. Our horses are friends and they're not leaving each other's side.

"Come on, Elizabeth." I gesture with my reins toward the far end of the beach. "Let's go!"

And off we ride. Through the water, down the golden beach with our family and friends all around us.

"This is so cool, Brandt," shouts Elizabeth, not looking scared any more.

I don't answer because my heart is racing with the thrill of riding a horse for the first time.

Doña Maria rides near us on her gentle horse. "Elizabeth," she calls. "Look at my fairy wings!" And there is Doña Maria's hair fallen from her bun and spread out on her shoulders, just like silvery wings.

"Tía, you look beautiful!" Elizabeth's horse, Pikachu, leaps over the foamy sea.

Just then, a passing cloud opens up in the sky and raindrops fall down in the warm, light drizzle I have become accustomed to on this island. Our horses don't seem to mind the rain one bit. They raise their hoofs high and prance around at the edge of the sea.

"Look, Brandt, our horses are dancing in the rain," says Elizabeth, sounding like a poem as usual. She's right. They do look like that. Dancing up and down the beach.

Grandfather rides by. "This was a perfect plan, Mister Brandt. Bravo!" Grand Pop looks happy. And not a small kind of happy, either.

"Thanks, Uncle David," I whisper to the sky.

As I keep holding on tightly to Amigo down the beach, I think about all of the tragedies that make our hearts hurt so much. That make us scared and sad and angry. But, still, there is joy. Because just look at us. Look at us all.

Elizabeth smiles at me like she understands what I'm thinking. This is our wish coming true for our mothers.

"You hear the sea?" asks Elizabeth. I look over at the shifting shades of blue that feels like home now.

"It's singing a happy sea song."

I try to hear what Elizabeth hears, but all I can really hear is the swishing of Amigo's tail and the glop glop glop sound of his hooves hitting the sand. Then, slowly, like a whistle from far away I hear the beginning of a song. But it's not the sea. It's Mommy. And she's singing one of her morning songs.

Jared hears her, too, and he looks back at me and grins. "You were right, Bubba."

"About what?" I shout at him.

"That Story of Everything you want to write – it'll even have horses."

Only Jared would remember that. I laugh as loudly as I dare without scaring Amigo. "Yes, it will."

About the Author

Photograph by Leslie Joseph

Lynn Joseph was born and raised in Trinidad and has used her childhood experiences in Trinidad and other Caribbean islands as her source of inspiration to develop her writing for children and young adults. Ms. Joseph is the author of numerous books for children, including *A Wave in Her Pocket*, *An Island Christmas*, *The Mermaid's Twin Sister*, *Jump Up Time: A Trinidad Carnival Story* and *The Color of My Words*. Her young adult novel, *Flowers in the Sky*, was published by HarperCollins in March, 2013.

Lynn was Bermuda's 2011 Writer in Residence and is the Editor of the Anthology, *I Wish I Could Tell You: Bermuda Anthology of Children's Literature and Young Adult Stories*. She is also an attorney, and recently, she graduated with a Masters of Fine Arts in Writing for Children & Young Adults from the Vermont College of Fine Arts in July 2014.

Her website is **www.lynnjosephauthor.com** for more information.

TALES FOR YOUNG ADULTS

FROM BLOUSE & SKIRT BOOKS

ALL OVER AGAIN
BY A-DZIKO SIMBA GEGELE
**Who Knew Growing up
Could be so Hard?**

GROWING UP IS HARD. You know this. And when your mother has X-ray eyes and dances like a wobbling bag of water? When your father's idea of fun is to put all your money in a savings account and make you get up at 5 am every Sunday morning? When Kenny, Percival Thorton High's big show-off, is after Christina Parker – your Christina Parker? And when you have a shrimp of a little sister who is the bawlingest little six year old girl in the whole of Riverland? Then growing up is something you not sure you can manage at all. Who in their right mind could? Who? You?

All Over Again is an enchanting slice of boyhood. It is a charming coming of age story with a bold narrative style that pulls you into it.

Winner of the 2014 Burt Award for Caribbean Literature and longlisted for the 2015 International IMPAC Dublin Literary Award.

TALES FOR YOUNG ADULTS

FROM BLOUSE & SKIRT BOOKS

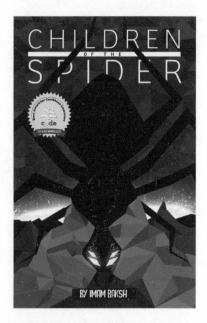

CHILDREN OF THE SPIDER
BY IMAM BAKSH
The Spiders are Coming!

MAYALI IS A GIRL on the run. Driven by desperation and the search for her father, Mayali leaves behind everything she has ever known on her home world of Zolpash, a land of sulphur and harsh weather, and journeys to Guyana. There she meets Joseph, a boy without the gift of speech but with much to say. Together they go on a daring, cross-country adventure to save earth from the invading Spider gods and their armies. Will their warning come too late? Will anyone even believe them? And will Mayali be able to find her father?

Children of the Spider is a fast-paced adventure. The story moves from the lush hinterlands of Guyana through to the bustling city of Georgetown where the colonial past continues to rub shoulders with the gritty, contemporary world. It is a refreshing take on Caribbean myth and mythology from an interesting new voice.

Children of the Spider won first place in the 2015 Burt Award for Caribbean Literature.